Teddy Bear Cannibal Massacre

Teddy Bear Cannibal Massacre

11 Stories of Fear, Obsession and Killer Clowns
Edited by Tim Lieder

Dybbuk Press
http://www.dybbuk-press.com
New York, NY

Library of Congress Control Number: 2005932130

ISBN: 0-9766546-0-1

First Edition: May 2005

Cover Art by Amanda Rehagen

Table of Contents

Formaldehyde
by C. C. Parker

Everything was leaking out of him; out of every pore. Terry was pretty fucking sick. Bad mushrooms. Bad high. He got outside just fast enough so as to not puke on his brother's carpet. Just the thought color swirling around his brain made him sick; made him think of Salvador Dali, Francis Bacon, Picasso. He'd wanted to be a painter himself at one time, but it had never been enough to sustain him.

"Shit, man . . . you okay?"

Terry hadn't seen Carl standing there.

"Too many," he said. "I told you."

"Fuck you, Carl!"

"Yeah . . . whatever."

"No, I mean it."

Terry left on one of his classic walks. He did this often when he was either too high or depressed to deal with the real world . . . not that Carl was a very good example. Carl was three years older than Terry, which really didn't make a whole hell of a lot of difference. When he came back Carl was watching a Bill Hicks video: Sane Man.

"Where'd you go?"

"I don't know . . . everywhere."

"You know what I thought about," said Carl. "When you were gone?"

"What?"

"That time in school when you refused to dissect that worm."

"It was a living thing," explained Terry.

"It was a worm shit-fuck."

"Bill Hicks is dead in ninety-four. Same as Kurt Cobain. The day the music died."

"What the fuck are you talking about?"

"That was the year."

Carl sprawled on the couch reading a battered horror novel. It made Terry think about all the stories his brother used to read him when they were kids. Mostly, they were stories about zombies; flesh eating bitches that sucked the brains out of their victims.

"You still reading that shit," he said.

"Fuck, dude . . . you scared me."

"I've only been standing there for the last five minutes."

"How you feeling?"

"A little queasy, still . . . I probably should force some food down."

"There's should be some juice . . . or beer, if you want."

Terry knew some dude in high school who thought he was a zombie. Lance Freed. Typical small town bullshit. He got busted for digging a body out of the graveyard with this metal head tweaker – Jack or Brad or who cares. They were both on acid. They cut the woman's head off, stuck a broom handle through her neck and set off across town in Lance's Camaro with it stuck out the window.

Terry sat on the couch with a red tumbler between his legs. Carl loaded a bowl, after he put on a *Simpsons* tapes. Terry'd been taping them since the second season.

"You were kind of out of your head last night."

"You were right."

"Fuck yeah, I was."

"All I could think about when I woke up was the worm."

"Jesus, I don't remember."

"You don't remember mentioning the worm?"

"Maybe."

"You ever smell formaldehyde?"

"You mean the shit coroners use to keep bodies fresh."

"The very same."

"Sure . . . What about it?"

"I could smell it last night. Like some kind of a relapse."

"Relapse to what?"

"The worm."

"Fuck man."

Terry like the way the Simpsons looked as a backdrop. He couldn't say much for reality these days. Maybe if he gave painting a serious shot it would make sense. Maybe not.

Just because he wouldn't kill a fucking worm.

"I gotta get out here," said Terry. "I told mom I'd go to the store for her."

"When are you gonna finally get your own place?"

"When there's a reason."

"Isn't not having to live with mom reason enough."

"I could move in with you."

"Bullshit, fucker . . . I earned my sovereignty."

"It's Alex that I get sick of." Alex, their step dad. Their real dad died in a logging accident when Terry was eleven. It had been the year of the worm. The same year that Lance Freed crept into the Marshfield Cemetery and dug Harriet Banks out of the ground. The year of the zombie.

"I started painting that year."

"What?"

"Nothing."

"Fuck, Terry . . . you need to dip your stick into some pussy or something. You're starting to worry me."

"I'll see you."

"Late."

On the way home, Terry half promised himself to quit doing so many drugs, but he was just bullshitting himself. Drugs helped sink him deeper into the abyss of himself. Stupid. He was stupid forever wanting to quit.

His mom was resting on the couch when he walked in.

"Terry," she said "I was half asleep."

"Sorry."

"Are you ready to go to the store."

"I guess."

"What do you mean 'I guess?'"

"Fine."

"I made a list." She got up awkwardly and lumbered to the kitchen. Her breath lingered heavy behind her. "If you want beer you'll have to buy it."

"What about Alex?"

"He wants you to take care of your own beer from now on."

"But he's always smoking my weed."

She handed him the list, which he crushed.

"What are you doing?"

"It's okay." He stuffed it in his pocket. She handed him three twenties.

"Can I at least get some cigarettes?"

"Only one pack."

Terry drove his mom's station wagon into town. Marshfield High School blurred past on his right, the cemetery settled gray beside it. His mother's breath had smelled like formaldehyde.

Safeway's door slid open. Seven cash registers rattled endlessly. It looked like the end of the world. People's carts were heaped with bounty; they would be

back in a week, and the week after that . . . unless
something stopped them. Maybe he had missed something;
a holiday, a war . . . anything that caused so much
confusion and avarice. It was Saturday. That's all that he
could think of.

He brought the items home and set them on the
table.

"Your brother called," said his mom.

"All right."

"Carl?"

"Hey, man."

"Mom said you called."

"I was just think about all that worm shit."

"What about it?"

"You said I mentioned it last night, but I don't
remember."

"Did you eat more?"

"Nah."

"I don't know what to say."

"They use that stuff you were talking about on dead
worms too; before they're dissected."

"Do you remember a dude named Lance Freed?"

"The guy that dug up that old lady and sliced her
head off. He used to mow her lawn. I think maybe he was
in love with her."

"That's fucked, man."

"A lot of shit is."

"Did you ever talk to him or anything?"

"Nah . . . he was a couple grades under me."

"So."

"I don't know . . . he seemed pretty fucking strange. I
heard he used to crack the skulls of cats and suck out their
brains."

"Fuck, Carl."

"You asked?"

"Whatever happened to him?"

"He killed himself, man . . . a week before they were going to put him away."

Terry remembered hearing something like it; a null extension of the eternal rumor. It seemed like bullshit; like the stuff in Carl's books. It wasn't.

"Do you believe in Zombies, Carl?"

"Nah."

"Cool . . . late."

"Late."

Click.

Doof Doof Doof
by Paul Haines

"Please don't take this the wrong way," she murmured, pretending to pick a piece of fluff from off his coat, "but I think I'm falling in love with you."

She left her hand upon his arm after she finished speaking, stroking him with short, delicate movements.

"You have no idea how long I've waited to hear those words," he said, as blood soared throughout his veins. He swam deep into the green grass of her eyes. The scent of her body, her perfume strong and seductive, her lips soft, red and full, her hair gold and shining in this perfect summer afternoon.

She moved closer, pressing against him, her bosom firm but yielding against his chest. He fought to control and hide his instant reaction.

She smiled shyly, moving her mouth inches from his own and whispered "Would it be too much to ask for a kiss?"

An orchestra of a thousand fluting birds piped into his brain, almost dizzy, blood rushing behind his eyes.

"Of course, my beloved Little Red Riding Hood," he replied, bending towards her, preparing finally to taste her tongue, to drink the sweet nectar from her lips.

"Oh, but wait," she said, stepping back from his arms. "Listen. Can you hear it?"

A low doof-doof-doof grew louder and louder, until the sound surrounded them, overwhelmingly powerful and deafening. Little Red Riding Hood began to dance wildly, throwing her arms and legs around maniacally, pumping her body to the beat.

Doof-Doof-Doof!

"I love this song!" she said jerking her head up and down. "Sorry Wolfie, gotta dance, Ciao!"

"Nnnooooo!!!!" screamed the Wolf. "Wait, wait! I'm so close, she loves me, she finally loves - "

Wolf awoke to the ceiling fan above him shuddering to the doof-doof heavy bass of music thudding through the walls of his apartment, the ecstasy of his dream ripped quickly from his head.

His raging hard-on rapidly failed as he glanced despondently towards his alarm clock.

"It's three in the fuckin' mornin'," he growled, climbing out of bed and throwing on a beaten old yellow bathrobe he'd stolen from Papa Bear's place a few months ago. And in case he had to venture out, he whipped on his kippa, and had to adjust the skullcap slightly as it slid upon his bald patch.

He bleared his way towards the kitchen, flicked on the light, grabbed a broom and beat futilely on the ceiling against the bubblegum squeak chanting soullessly to the thudding beats.

Ooh Baby, boogie baby, yeah yeah yeah,
Everybody, everyone, yeah yeah yeah.

"Turn that shit down!" he screamed, bashing the ceiling with the broom again, punching little round holes into the plaster.

Ooh baby, yeah baby, yeah yeah yeah.

Wolf shook his head in despair, eyeing the half eaten chickens strewn around his lounge floor, the beard of mould that grew stubbornly and silently across his kitchen bench, and his grubby, disheveled, barely rooted-on, double-bed. This wasn't the best place in the world, hell all it needed was some new wallpaper really and maybe a bit of a clean, but this was where he called home. His fucking home for Christ's sake! All he could afford if he wanted to live anywhere near Little Red Riding, who had the Penthouse suite in the very same building.

"But I can't fuckin" stalk her if I can't get any fuckin" sleep!" he yelled, pounding the ceiling.

Doof doof doof.

Yeah baby yeah baby

"Fuck you!" he howled, swinging the broom into the cordless phone on the wall next to Miss December. It splintered into little black pieces of plastic across the brown and orange checkered lino. He'd been disconnected last week for not paying his bill.

Not much satisfaction though.

Doof doof doof.

Not much at all.

He opened the cupboard beneath the sink. Shoving aside some old plates caked in grime, he found a fried egg sporting greenish veins over the yolk. Pleasantly surprised, he peeled it from the congealed fat in the roasting dish and popped it into his mouth and then pulled out his trusty crowbar from behind garbage bags he'd filled and discarded some weeks back.

He felt reassured with the cold weight in his hand. Made of tungsten too. Heavy duty, twice the cost and worth every cent. He knew where that beat was coming from.

Wolf stormed out of his apartment, slamming the door behind him. He marched up the stairs to the third floor, nostrils flaring, a mistake as the stairwell stunk of stale dwarf vomit and piss. Those little bastards must have crept in through the fire escape door again.

He threw open the third floor entry door and stomped down the hallway towards the noise. For sure, this time *he* would be the hero.

Doof doof doof.

This sort of carry-on was unacceptable, especially mid-week. Good God, this racket would even wake Little Red Riding Hood, asleep in her Penthouse suite. Maybe she'd thank him for this later, this heroic deed of his. Yeah, maybe she would.

Christ, he'd almost kissed her. And then that bloody music had woken him up just as he - just as – it was just too much.

Wolf watched the walls vibrating as he stood outside the guilty apartment. On the wooden door a gold plaque proclaimed to the world "412". Big gold lock. Tiny silver peephole.

He thumped on the door.

Doof doof doof.

He thumped again trying to thump his thumps between the drumbeat, but the bpms were too fast.

"Little Pig, Little Pig," Wolf yelled, cracking the crowbar against the door, "Let me come in!"

The music grew louder.

"Right then," he muttered under his breath, and swung the crowbar into the door. This baby would even rip through brick. Special designs for special purposes. He grinned, and swung again. The door splintered and Wolf laughed, ripping away large strips of wood with the crowbar, his energy high, his blood boiling.

And behind the wooden door stood another, a door of thick solid steel. Cold, hard, unrelenting steel. Impenetrable.

Wolf stood there stunned; defeat rose in his mind, eroding the anger infused in his limbs. He howled and beat upon the steel door with the last of his strength, steel on steel clanging, bouncing from wall to wall down the hallway, staccato with his sobbing.

Broken, Wolf ceased his hammering and faced the distant stairwell. It's what's always happened, he thought bitterly. To his father, to his grandfather, and to his father before him. An endless cycle of losers, eventually beaten down and whipped.

Suddenly the volume went down. He heard bolts being drawn from behind thick inches of steel. It opened silently, ominously and a high pitched voice squealed from behind it.

"Hey guys, I think the pizzas are here."

A savage grin crept across Wolf's visage.

A pig wearing a bright blue shirt thrust his head out the door. His eyes were unfocused, the pupils dilated.

"Hey, you ain't the pizza guy!" said Stupid Pig.

Wolf saw flecks of white powder crystallizing in the snot dripping from Stupid Pig's nostrils. He remembered smashing down Stupid Pig's wire-mesh fly-screen door last year and beating the shit out of him for late night drug parties. Thought he'd fucked off since then.

"Nope, I'm not the pizza guy, but I got something for you anyway," Wolf growled, pushing Stupid Pig back through the doorway and clubbing him around the head with the crowbar.

Stupid Pig fell to the floor, already unconscious, and Wolf put in the boot until blood leaked from Stupid Pig's ears.

Feeling invincible, Wolf strode into the room and stopped speechless, his heart frozen, the scene in the room burned in his brain. His first instinct was to tear them limb from limb, but he knew he couldn't. It wasn't allowed according to the scriptures.

Little Pig lay grinning, sprawled naked on the rotating king-size four-poster bed. He was handcuffed to the headposts. Little Red Riding Hood, clad only in her satin red cloak, kneeled over him, her head bobbing up and down over Little Pig's groin. Little Pig squealed in delight thrusting upwards, ever upwards.

Fat Pig grunted frantically, thrusting his fat little hips against Little Red Riding Hood's arse as he fucked her from behind. His body was slick with sweat, he looked like he had been at it for a long time.

Wolf could hear Little Red Riding Hood moaning with every thrust, as Fat Pig porked her, and Wolf threw up over himself and began choking.

"What the fuck?" said Little Pig, noticing Wolf for the first time.

Fat Pig kept pumping.

"Oh sweet Jesus," wept Wolf as he attempted to wipe the spew matting his chest fur. This couldn't be happening, he must still be dreaming. The vomit burning in his nose assured him that he was, in fact, wide and horribly awake.

"What you doon here?" slurred Little Pig. "You want some this?"

"Hey, no weird shit," said Little Red Riding Hood, unhinging her jaw from Little Pig's loins. "No inter-racial stuff. That costs extra. And turn that music back up, I love that song."

Wolf watched in horror as his own fingers turned the dial on the stereo back up.

Doof doof doof.

Fat Pig kept pumping, pumping, pumping...

Wolf wandered dejectedly back towards his room. His mind was closing down. Blotting out everything, everyone, his emotions, his feelings, his love, his hatred. There was no point, none at all. She had been his reason to live. Fuck this. He'd save them the trouble. He'd go the same way as his old man. Christ, if only pork was *kosher*!

He staggered into his bathroom and filled the cauldron he'd pinched off the witch in the forest with cold water. He hadn't paid the bills. He found a match and lit the coals beneath the cauldron and climbed on in and waited for it to boil.

It was a stupid way to die he realized, watching the surface of the water ripple with every doof-doof beat.

Peppercorn Rent
by Roberta Rogow

"Miss Lupine, may I have a word?"

Susi Lupine stopped half-way down the stairs that led to her small but precious hideaway, an attic room in a late-Victorian row house in Kensington. Her landlord, Major Patrick Wetherby stood at the foot of the stairs, his mighty Guardsman's mustache drooping apologetically.

"What's up?" Susi sniffed the air, expecting breakfast. There was no aroma of frying sausage, no burnt toast, not even the hum of the tea-urn. Clearly, something was definitely wrong with the world when the Wetherbys did not prepare the classic British Breakfast.

Major Wetherby was joined by his wife, a rotund woman with a perpetually worried frown. "It's the rent, dear."

"I thought we'd agreed on that. I've already paid you ten pounds for the month." Susi started down the stairs once more.

"Not yours, dear. Ours." Mrs. Wetherby stifled a sniffle of agony.

"We've received notice," the third member of the Wetherby family said gloomily. Jan Wetherby, the Major's son, was the reason Susi had found her digs; a lanky young man usually decked out in ostentatiously grubby jeans and leather jacket, when he was not forced into the suit demanded by Yates and Bates Insurance. Jan and Susi had struck up a friendship at Yates and Bates, based on the fact that each had something to hide. Jan had confided his loathing of insurance sales and his desire to join Susi in her relentless pursuit of insurance fraud. Susi had not been quite so forthcoming, but had hinted at an obscure medical problem that made her a difficult tenant, one who tended to roam at night and make odd noises once a month. Jan had mentioned that his parents had a spare room at the top of their house, which might be rented for a small sum, and the bargain had been struck.

Susi followed her hosts into the dark dining room. "What's all this about? I thought this house was yours, free and clear."

"Not quite," Jan said. "The house is Dad's, but the land isn't."

"The land?" Susi's eyes narrowed. "Is this some kind of Brit thing? You own the house, but not the land it's built on?"

"The land itself is part of Lord Aspern's estate," Ma Wetherby quavered.

"And now the bloody bastard wants his rent. His full rent!" Major Wetherby picked up a document. Susi appropriated it and scanned it.

" 'I will arrive at seven o'clock, as per the agreement of 1485, to collect the Peppercorn Rent due me.' " Susi shrugged. "I don't see what all the fuss is about. Just give this guy his pepper, or whatever it is he's supposed to get..."

"You don't understand, Miss Lupine," Major Wetherby said. "We can't give him the rent. It's the Agreement of 1485."

Susi's dark eyes narrowed. Her nose seemed sharper and longer in the darkened room. "Just what's involved in this agreement?"

"It's said that the first Lord Aspern was fleeing after Bosworth. He'd managed to betray both sides, and wanted to hide out until the dust died down," Major Wetherby explained. "So he took shelter in what was then a small farmstead, just outside London...."

"Here?" Susi guessed.

Major Wetherby nodded. "Precisely. At that time, this place was an out-of-the-way nondescript bit of English countryside."

"Times do change," Susi commented. The Wetherby residence was now in the very heart of Kensington, where Princess Di could once be seen doing her daily shopping.

"So the farmer hid Lord Aspern in his daughter's bed. Once Aspern made it up with Henry Tudor, he got the farmstead as a reward, and showed his gratitude to the farmer by remitting the exorbitant rent he usually demanded and insisted only that the daughter of the house spend the night with him, on request. It's called a Peppercorn Rent. " That seemed to be enough explanation for the Wetherby clan. Susi was not satisfied.

"Let me get this straight," she said slowly. "This Aspern character expects someone..."

"'The daughter of the house, or her equivalent'," Major Wetherby quoted.

"Some girl is supposed to spend the night with this...this..."

"Exactly so." The family gazed at the notice with foreboding.

Susi shook her head in disbelief at British traditions. "But this place isn't an old family home," she pointed out. "You got it when you retired from the Army. It's not as if you're bound to this lord, like a medieval serf."

"We're not. The house is. Whoever owns the house, or resides in the house, is responsible to Lord Aspern for the rent," the Major explained.

Susi was still unconvinced.

"What happens if there isn't a daughter, or someone willing to do spend the night with this creep?" Susi's American brain tried to grasp all the ramifications of the situation.

"Aspern forecloses, and we lose our home," Mrs. Wetherby moaned.

`"And I'm back out on the street," Susi said to herself. This would be a greater disaster than any of the Wetherbys knew. Susi had managed to keep her monthly indisposition a secret from her hosts for almost a year. To find another household both convenient to an open space and cheap enough for her to afford on what Yates and Bates paid her would be a nightmare. Relocating back to the States was out of the question. Clearly, something had to be done!

"Why hasn't this Lord Aspern asked for his rent until now?" Susi wanted to know.

"Because he's a new chap," Jan explained. "The old man was quite gaga, and let his solicitor make all the arrangements for him."

"And he was satisfied with twenty-five pounds a year just to keep the tax-man at bay and claim this property as a dead loss," Major Wetherby added. "Now this fellow comes along from America, the grandson of the old lord, and he's decided to call in all the old deeds."

"It was in the newspapers," Mrs. Wetherby pointed out. "He's going around London, picking up all the little bits and pieces of land that kings gave to the lords of Aspern, nothing big enough to build a manor or a castle on, just a lot here and there."

"Why?" Susi asked, her long nose twitching. She could almost smell a fraud somewhere, one of the few advantages of her unusual metabolism.

"Because none of the Asperns were worth the shot to blow them to Hell!" Major Wetherby roared. "Including Lord Derrek. This chap's father. I served with him as a lad, in the Suez crisis. He went to America, married some starlet, and drank himself to death in California."

"I mean, why does this Lord Aspern want all these little bits of land that no one really can use for anything except houses like this one?" Susi elucidated.

"If we knew that, we might be able to come to another arrangement, like the one we had with the old gentleman," Major Wetherby said.

Susi's brows contracted in thought. "What happens if there is no one to spend the night with Lord Aspern? I mean, suppose there is no daughter in the household?" Susi pursued the problem. "It's been five hundred years. You can't tell me that every time one of these Asperns came calling there was a girl willing to go and spend the night with him."

"I suppose a substitute could be provided," Jan said. "As for willing girls, there were plenty of them in Tudor and Stuart times I imagine. It would be an honor, really." He smiled brightly at his parents, who did not return the look. "Of course, the custom died out in the last century. Who did it last, do you know?"

Major Wetherby pulled at his mustache. "I've no idea. We took the place when old Mandeville was put into the Chelsea Home. Old Lord Aspern's solicitor came around and told us about the peppercorn rent, and said we'd never have to pay it, since the old gentleman was long past demanding it."

"And this Aspern creep is coming tonight?" Susi's frown lifted, and her eyes started to glitter. Her lips curled in a smile that showed her sharp, white teeth.

"Tonight," Jan said, consulting the letter. "He's coming around at seven o'clock, to collect the daughter of the house or the deed, whichever comes first." Jan looked at their paying guest, and blanched. "You don't mean... You wouldn't ..."

Major Wetherby harrumphed into his mustache. "I really can't ask. . ."

Jan recognized the glint in his colleague's eyes. She had that look when she read spec sheets and claims forms. It usually meant that someone was going to pay dearly. "Oh, Susi, I can't let you do this. I mean, you don't know this chap at all. He might do something terrible to you."

Susi patted her friend's cheek. "Jan, you and your family have been very kind to me while I've been here in London. I didn't have a place to stay, and you took me in. You've put up with my comings and goings, and the rent is very reasonable, and so's the food. It's the least I can do to pay you back for all the help you've given me." Besides, she thought to herself, I owe it to modern womanhood to teach this twerp a lesson he'll never forget! And I think there's something very fishy in this sudden urge to collect London real estate. This Aspern is after something, I know it, and I'm going to find out what it is.

Jan flushed red under his straggling beard. Major Wetherby harrumphed. Mrs. Wetherby smiled weakly.

"Then that's settled," Susi said. "Now, Mrs. Wetherby, could I have some breakfast, please? I'm ravenous!"

At that very moment, in his luxurious suite at the Dorchester Hotel, the dark-haired, slightly-built fortyish man who had so recently inherited the title of Lord Aspern was ingesting his own breakfast, while his scruffy companion in crime, Tommy Belton, went over his mail with him.

"One more lot taken care of," Belton said, tossing an official-looking envelope at his ostensible boss. "But I'm damned if I know what you want all these bits of land for. None of 'em are big enough to build anything on."

Reginald Napier, Lord Aspern, added jam to his buttered toast and shoveled the whole into his mouth. He washed it down with a cup of tea, wiped jam off his chin, and regarded his henchman with pitying eyes.

"Those so-called bits and pieces are exactly the right size for American fast-food franchisers," he explained. "Have you any idea how much the Bonnie Burger Corporation will pay for a bit of Britain? Especially in the middle of London?"

"Ah." Light dawned. "So you pick up the deeds to the land..."

"And the Americans pay a rent that will keep both of us in the South of France for years to come," Aspern gloated. "In dollars, not peppers, either. Tomorrow I can sign away all the deeds to one..." he consulted the papers on the table."...Jeffrey Jellicoe,Jr."

Belton frowned over his cup. It could have been the difficulties of thought, or his opinion of British coffee. "But what about this Wetherby bit? The one in Kensington?"

"Oh, yes, the peppercorn rent. I've had my lawyers looking into that. It's legal, all right, only there is no 'daughter of the house'. The residents are Major and Mrs. Wetherby and their son, Jan."

"Don't suppose you'd fancy the lad," Belton sniggered.

Aspern glared icily at him. "No, I would not. And the agreement of 1485 specifies the daughter of the house, not the son."

"What about tonight?" Belton asked, with a leer. "Champagne and caviar, or just tea and cookies?"

"Tonight," Aspern mused, "you may book me a table at the Ritz for dinner. Then I'll take in a night spot or two..."

"There's a new place over the river. Just called The Club. Really hot stuff." Belton offered. "All the top people go there. They've even got a hot new singer, if you can call it that. Lime Green Jello."

"I suppose I might look in on it," Aspern said. "Get the car, Belton. I'm going to look over my properties."

"What about the Wetherby rent?"

"I'll be at their door at seven sharp. By five minutes after, they should have been served with their notice to dispossess. By seven-thirty, I shall be at the Ritz." Aspern considered his wardrobe. "Shall I wear the Kenzo or the Armani...?"

"To the Ritz or The Club?" Belton responded.

"Either."

"Armani'll do for the Ritz," Belton said, snaffling up the bits of breakfast left on the plates. "The Club's more grunge."

"I can change after dinner," Aspern decided. "Plenty of time, and I can pick up someone at The Club for afters."

"But suppose they've got a peppercorn rent girl at the Wetherby place?" Belton persisted.

"They won't," Aspern said confidently. "And I can close the deal with Jellicoe, Junior tomorrow, and be off to the South of France the next day."

Visions of white beaches and tanned bodies danced in his head as he donned a carefully tailored suit for the day's activities.

"Are you sure you want to go through with this?" Jan asked for the fortieth time, as he watched Susi preen before the hall mirror. The American girl had poured herself into a little black dress, which fitted her athletic body like the proverbial glove. Her hair, usually left to fly about her head, had been carefully coifed for the occasion, and was wound into a super-chic chignon, anchored with gold pins. She had even tortured her feet into her one and only pair of high heels.

"When am I ever going to spend the night with a Lord again?" Susi asked impishly. "Oh, don't look so serious, Jan. All the agreement says is 'spend the night'. It doesn't say what we do together."

"That was understood," Jan said stuffily.

"But it's not in writing," Susi pointed out. "Besides, I think there's something weird about this whole setup. Jan, you're always nagging me about being let in on the Insurance Frauds team. Why don't you use that dandy little computer of yours and find out just what Lord Aspern's land grab is really about?"

"But what about. . ."

"Don't you worry about me, sugar. I can take care of myself!" Susi grinned toothily.

Mrs. Wetherby had been keeping watch at the front window. Now she dithered up the stairs to Susi's bedroom. "Oh, dear me, he's here!"

A huge and glossy Rolls-Royce limousine sailed around the corner and into the street. Lace curtains twitched as astonished neighbors got their fill of the show.

Belton, in a grubby chauffeur's uniform, emerged, to hold the door for Lord Aspern. The short but dapper landlord had decked himself out in a tuxedo, ready for his evening's amusements. He mounted the steps to the Wetherby front door, noting the proximity of the site to the street. Bonnie Burgers would be delighted, he thought. A perfect location, right in the middle of a quiet neighborhood, within walking distance of the schools and shops, in sight of Kensington Palace. Maybe they could get Princess Anne to the opening...

Visions of Paradise danced in his head as he knocked at the door. They were shattered by the sight of an attractive young woman, obviously dressed for a night on the town. At her feet rested a small leather satchel, contents to be surmised.

"You must be Lord Aspern," the girl said cheerfully. "I'm Susi Lupine. Your peppercorn rent," she added, as he stared blankly at her.

"Do come in, Lord Aspern," Jan said, as Lord Aspern stepped into the murky parlor.

"I was under the impression...." Aspern began,

"That there was no 'daughter of the house'," Jan said smoothly. "In which case, of course, you would be entitled to foreclose."

"Yes, that was the general idea," Aspern said. He took in the shabby furnishings of the parlor, and smiled genially at the Major and Mrs. Wetherby, as they huddled together in the parlor entrance.

"There have been, um, recent developments," Jan went on. "May I offer you something before you and Miss Lupine leave?"

Aspern frowned. "Wait just a minute," he snapped. "Just who is this Miss Lupine? The terms of the agreement are quite clear. The person who spends the night must be a 'daughter of the house'. When did Miss Lupine join your family?"

Susi put her arm through Jan's and laid her head on his shoulder. "Jan and I are going to be married," she said, with a toothy smile. "Dad and Mum Wetherby look on me as a daughter, don't you, you dear old things?"

Mum tottered out from behind the parlor draperies. "Oh, yes, Susi is just like one of our own," she agreed.

"Good gal," Major Wetherby added.

Aspern looked dubiously from Susi to Jan. "Well, if it suits you, I suppose..." He gallantly offered his arm to Susi. "I had a table booked for one at the Ritz, but I suppose they can find another chair."

Jan kissed Susi chastely on the cheek. "Be a good girl," he said.

Susi winked as she was handed into the limousine by the ever-present Belton.

"Don't worry, darlings, " she called out, to the delight of the neighbors and the mortification of the Wetherby's, "I'll be back, safe and sound, tomorrow. Cinderella's going to the ball!"

Belton glanced at the happy couple as he careened down Brompton Road towards the more fashionable dining spots of London. Lord Aspern glanced at Susi from time to time, assessing her possibilities. He preferred pneumatic baby-faced blondes, whose IQ matched their bust size. Sharp-witted, sharp-faced brunettes were usually too clever for him, and he despised anyone more clever than he. On her part, Susi was more and more convinced that this Lord Aspern had some reason for demanding his peppercorn rent. Between them, she and Jan would find out what it was, expose it, and get rid of him.

They both began to speak at the same time.

"When did you become Lord Aspern?" Susi asked, just as Aspern said, "And when did you and Mr. Wetherby meet, Miss Lupine?"

"I'm sorry, Lord Aspern," Susi said, with a nervous giggle.

"Oh...call me Reggie," Aspern said gallantly. "Until last year, I didn't even know I had a grandfather, let alone one with a title. My mother never said much about my dad, except that he had a taste for women and whiskey, and knew a good land deal when he saw one."

"All of which I'm sure you inherited," Susi murmured.

Aspern went on, "I'm quite fascinated by this engagement of yours. It wasn't announced in the newspapers, or banns posted, or anything like that."

"Well, we haven't really set the date," Susi said. "See, we both work for the same insurance company, and they don't like it when two employees marry. One of them has to leave, and neither of us really wants to."

"How short-sighted of them," Aspern said. His brain was ticking away. Perhaps he could get the land with a spot of blackmail. As it was, the south of France was slipping through his fingers with every minute he spent with this wretched girl.

Susi clutched at his arm. "Oh, you wouldn't say anything, would you? Because if you did, we'd have to break our engagement."

"I wouldn't want you to do that," Aspern crooned. He looked out the window, expecting to see the Edwardian architecture of the Ritz Hotel. Instead, he was affronted by a garish display of neon tubing wreathing a door painted an aggressive orange.

"Belton!"

The henchman turned in his seat to gaze at his boss. "Something wrong?"

"Where are we?"

"You said the Ritz. Best new restaurant in London. Favorite of all the stars. Says so in the Michelin Guide."

"I meant the restaurant at the Ritz Hotel, not some gimcrack hang-out for the Rich and Famous." Aspern regarded the line at the door, then smiled weakly at Susi, who smiled gamely back. "Well, I hope they can find us a table for two. I wasn't expecting company, Miss Lupine."

"I'll bet you weren't," Susi said to herself. Aloud she said, "You can call me Susi."

Aspern smiled with false sweetness at Susi, and mouthed over her head, "Do something!"

"When do you want me back?" Belton asked, ignoring the pleas of his putative employer.

Aspern's ferocious stare would have incinerated any lesser mortal. Belton had put up with far worse over the years, and was by now immune to his boss's tantrums.

"Ah...after dinner," Aspern said, trying to ignore the infamous satchel, which remained in the car.

"I'll give ya two hours, then I'll be around," Belton announced, removing the limo and any chance for Aspern to escape. All of London (at least, the London that Mattered) wanted to get into the Ritz. There was nothing to do but go forward. Somewhere in the back of his mind, Reginald Napier, Lord Aspern heard the voices of his noble forbears exhorting him. He would have to be bold, firm, and resolute, and get rid of this girl before the night was out, so that he could break that peppercorn rent and claim what was his (or what would be 'Bonnie Burgers').

The trouble with fashionable eating-spots, Aspern decided, was that they were full of people. The table he had booked so carefully in advance was not ready, and the duo had to sit in the bar for half an hour, nibbling salted snacks and watching the Rich and Famous being let in ahead of them. It took at least three tries before the maitre d'hôte approached the cheerful couple, since Lime Green Jello and his entire entourage, two film stars, and a Minor Royal had precedence over a mere Lord and his date. The joint was jumping, but the staff wasn't, and Susi and Aspern were shoved into a back corner while The Beautiful People claimed the attention of every waiter and barman in the place. By the time the waiter arrived, Susi was ready to eat anything, including her reluctant host. She settled for rack of lamb.

Aspern looked about, seeking a means of escape. Unfortunately, they were hemmed in by Lime Green Jello and his rock band, who were celebrating their newest record deal with champagne. Every time Aspern tried to excuse himself, an oddly-dressed person of indeterminate

sex pressed a glass on him and demanded that he drink to
the success of Lime Green Jello. Aspern smiled weakly and
complied, since lifting heavy electronic equipment and
smashing guitars onstage had given the band members and
the groupies impressive upper body development. Lime
Green Jello himself was on the scrawny side, but he made
up for it in sheer lung power.

On her part, Susi kept glancing at her watch, making
calculations based on the local astronomical tables. For a
moment she wondered if what she was about to spring on
her host was a little over the top, but then she decided that
he should be taught a lesson in manners. This was not
1485, and peppercorn rents were decidedly passe. Besides,
there was every indication that he had not intended to keep
his end of the bargain in the first place. He had only
ordered a table for one, and he had that hunted look in his
eye. She could smell the pheromones that inevitably
indicated that someone was lying. Susi smiled at her host,
and tried to listen to what he was saying over the roar of
the crowd.

"Why did you decide to demand your peppercorn
rent?" Susi asked her date. "I mean, Daddy Wetherby said
that your grandfather never even bothered to ask about it,
and took a token sum every year. I just can't understand
why you'd want to put those nice people out of their home.
You seem like a reasonable man, Reggie. Why don't you
just let them pay a nominal sum per year, like everyone
else, instead of this silly medieval peppercorn nonsense?"

"Tradition," was all that Aspern could come up with.
Luckily, the dessert cart arrived at the same time.

Aspern shuddered at his peppercorn rent's
voracious appetite. She worked her way through a trifle
and followed it with a slice of blackberry crumble. He tried
to remove himself, but once again Lime Green Jello
forestalled him.

"Can't leave the little lady, mate!" caroled the leader, in his best faux- Aussie accent. Aspern was hauled back to the table to pay his bill. Susi checked the time once again. She was beginning to get an all too familiar tingly feeling. For her plan to work, they had to have some privacy.

"Reggie, isn't it time for us to get back to your hotel?" she coaxed him.

Belton was waiting back at the limousine. "Thought you'd dumped her by now," Belton whispered, as Aspern helped insert Susi into the car.

"Not a hope," Aspern hissed.

Susi smiled brightly, and tapped the satchel with her toe. "Where to now?" she asked.

Aspern looked at Belton for an answer. . . any answer. "The Club's got a new band," Belton announced. "Some weird dessert name,...."

"Lime Green Jello?" Susi asked.

"That's it!"

"Why, we just had dinner with them," Aspern said. He turned to Susi. "The night's still young. Let's go dancing!"

"Dancing?" Susi quavered. This was cutting it close! Of course, she'd have to be near a window for her plan to work, so a dance hall sounded safe enough.

"Dancing," Aspern decided. In the general ruck of a dance hall he could lose his peppercorn rent, blame her for getting cold feet, and dispossess the Wetherby's the next morning.

It took some time for Belton to navigate through the medieval streets of the City of London, and get over the bridge. There, the Rolls joined the queue in front of the former warehouse in the seedy district on the wrong side of the Thames. Even if there hadn't been a mob scene in the narrow lane leading to the door, no one could miss the place. The walls were covered with orange and green paint, the door was plastered with used postage stamps, and the skylights were open to reveal the clear, starry sky.

"Whoever owns this joint must be making a mint," Susi observed, as she saw the throng lined up at the door.

The large tattooed individual at the door looked at the two in their oh-so-proper attire and turned up his nose. "Too old!" he decreed, sneering at Aspern. Then he checked Susi out, in her skin-tight black dress. "You pass." He lifted the rope to let Susi in.

"What! I'll have you know..." Aspern fumed.

"Maybe we should go somewhere more...private?" Susi hinted. The moon would rise at any minute, and she didn't want to be in the open when it did.

She was distracted by a burst of applause as another party arrived.

"It's you!" caroled Lime Green Jello.

"Can't get away from us, can you?" Susi said,.

"You know these people?" The bouncer asked suspiciously.

"We just dined together," Aspern told him.

"In a manner of speaking," Susi added.

Lime Green Jello nodded and winked. "Let 'em in," he told the bouncer.

They passed through into the vast interior of the Club. Apparently, ambiance was nothing, noise was everything to the Young and Bored. Susi wished she had brought her earplugs. Even without Lime Green Jello the din was spectacular, rendering conversation useless, if not impossible. The Club catered to the young and grungy, with various legal and illegal substances flowing copiously. The air was wreathed with smoke, some of which was tobacco. Black was the color of the evening, rendered in leather, lace, and shredded denim. Susi amused herself by counting the number of nose, navel and nipple rings she could spot, while Aspern checked out the exits and entrances, with an eye to possible escape from this howling hell.

"Why don't I find us some drinks?" Aspern tried to edge away from his unwanted date.

"I'd better go with you, or we'll get separated in this crowd." Susi grabbed his arm and held on like grim death.

"That was the general idea," Aspern muttered, as he shoved through a mass of writhing bodies to a long table at one end of the room.

The band on the platform in the middle of the room came to a screeching finale.

"And now....Lime Green Jello!" boomed out from the many speakers that decked the walls.

Lime Green Jello took his place at the microphone, his guitar slung somewhere in the vicinity of his crotch. Aspern wriggled out of Susi's grasp, with every intention of heading for the door and freedom. Overhead, the stars shone through the skylight of the former factory....and the moon shone with them.

Susi felt that monthly tingle in her fingers and toes as the moonlight touched her. Her skin grew hot and hairy, while her hands turned into paws with long, sharp nails. She could feel a tail emerging, thrusting through her underwear. Her dress was strangling her, and she writhed out of it, leaving the once-elegant garment to be trampled underfoot by combat boots and stiletto heels. Her face elongated into a muzzle. Her teeth grew long and sharp. Her vision blurred, colors receding, until her world was black and white and shades of gray. At the same time the odors in the tightly-packed room seemed to explode into her brain. Body secretions, burning tobacco and cannabis, even more exotic scents drove her into a frenzy. She pointed her muzzle to the open skylight and let out a howl of sheer delight, as Lime Green Jello whanged into his first number.

The overtones of the guitar slid upwards, past the range of human hearing. Susi's sensitive ears twitched in pain, and she let out another howl.

All around her, the crowd of dancers gazed in astonishment, adding their voices to hers. They didn't know what it was, but they wanted to be part of whatever was going on. They had never seen anything like this before, and they didn't want to miss a thing.

Susi leaped onto the stage, slavering and snarling. Lime Green Jello was enthralled. He worked himself into a frenzy of guitar glissandos and keyboard-crashing chords, while Susi yowled and pawed the air. The Young and the Bored were bored no more! They imitated her every move, thrashing and snarling, clawing the air and generally rampaging around the transfixed Aspern, who suddenly realized what he had escaped. "She knew!" he said aloud, to the unhearing crowd.

It suddenly occurred to him that now was as good a time as any to remove himself from The Club. He edged out of the crowd, and ran for the door....just as the police crashed in.

"This place is closed, by order of Her Majesty's Government..." intoned the Chief Inspector in charge of the raid.

"Whatever for?" Aspern queried.

"Drugs," snapped the nearest constable.

"But I'm Lord Aspern...."

"Then you should be ashamed of yourself, running about like a teenager," the constable scolded him.

Aspern found himself bundled into a police van with the rest of the lot, carted off to the local police station, and booked. His only consolation was that Susi was not with him, ergo, he could now claim that the peppercorn rent had not been received, and he could still seize the Wetherby property. Bonnie Burgers was within his grasp.

A snarling, howling, writhing Something jumped into the van with him.

"What the Hell...!" Aspern gasped.

"Is this your dog?" A policewoman gave him the look one gives a child molester. "Fancy bringing a fine animal to a place like that!"

Aspern shook his head in disbelief. Susi Lupine was not giving up! If, indeed, that WAS Susi Lupine. . . Aspern closed his eyes and wished desperately that his grandfather had never left him this ridiculous legacy.

It was a long, long night for Lord Aspern. He was fingerprinted, mug-shot, and herded into a waiting room with the rest of the Club's clientele, including Susi Lupine, who seemed to have returned, minus the Little Black Dress. The police matron found a shapeless cotton garment with which to cover her trim body. Aspern cowered in a corner as one by one the participants in the Club's arcane rituals were questioned, tested for illicit substance ingestion, and led to the telephone, where they could contact their lawyers or parents to come and get them out in the morning. Somewhere around three AM Aspern was permitted to call the Dorchester, and give Belton his instructions.

It was dawn when Belton arrived, carrying a suit on a hanger for Lord Aspern and the satchel for Susi Lupine. Behind him loomed Jan Wetherby and a short, stout man in a soberly-cut suit who turned out to be Lord Aspern's solicitor, Mr. Dawson.

"I thought you might need this," Belton explained, handing the boss more acceptable clothing than the now-rumpled Armani tuxedo.

"And I thought Miss Lupine might need this," Jan added, handing over the satchel.

Once the legal formalities had been concluded, Lord Aspern stepped out of the police station and into a blaze of light that had nothing to do with the rising sun.

"Lord Aspern? What were you doing at the Club?" yelled one of the reporters.

"Dancing?" Aspern stammered out. He stared wildly around for help.

Before he could go any farther, the Press found more interesting meat for the daily tabloids. "It's Lime Green Jello!"

All thoughts of Lord Aspern were thrown to the winds, as the Press converged on the Man of the Hour. A tall woman in a severely-cut Power Suit emerged from the crowd and took charge.

"That's enough, boys," she instructed the Fourth Estate. "Lime Green was just performing at The Club. He has no other connection with it. Make sure you get that part straight."

She marched forward and hissed, "Remember, we've got a very important deal to close!" Lime Green Jello shrugged and started down the street, the Press in hot pursuit.

"Hey, Lime Green! Do you know this bird?" someone at the back of the crowd yelled.

"She's the wildest dancer in London!" Lime Green exclaimed.

"Ah...I must have been under the influence of someone else's smoke," Susi said quickly. "But thanks, Lime."

"You can call me Jeff," Lime Green Jello told her. "And any time you get tired of this wimp, you can tour with us."

"Now there's an offer I can refuse," Susi said, as Jan and Aspern closed in around her and Mr. Dawson shooed the rest of the Press away. Belton drove through the mob,

and headed the limo towards Kensington and the
Wetherby house.

The neighbors got another eyeful when the Rolls
turned the corner and Aspern, Dawson, Jan and Susi
emerged and marched into the house, where the Wetherby
family was waiting in the front room to greet the returning
heroine.

"We spent the night together," Susi declared. "Of
course, we had some company, but I'd say the terms of the
peppercorn rent were fulfilled."

"Now wait just one minute, young woman!" Aspern
snapped out peevishly.

Jan smiled down upon his landlord. There were
times when a six-inch difference in height came in useful,
and this was one of them.

"While you and Miss Lupine were cavorting all over
London..." he began.

"We were not cavorting," Aspern objected. "We
were dining and dancing."

"Well, I was dancing," Susi admitted. "I think." She
rarely remembered anything she had done during her
monthly bouts of moonstruck mayhem.

"As I said," Jan continued, disregarding the
interruption, "I have been doing some research into this
peppercorn rent of ours. Computers are wonderful things
for research," he added, with a condescending smile at
Lord Aspern and a wink at Susi.

"And...?" Major Wetherby asked anxiously.

"It seems that if the peppercorn rent is not paid, and
the landlord refuses to accept the alternate rent, the land
escheats to the Crown," the solicitor explained.

"You mean I can't sell it to Bonnie Burgers after all?"
wailed Aspern.

"You son of a bitch!" Major Wetherby turned on him.

"Oh, you've met my mother, have you?" Aspern commented.

The Major was not to be deflected. "Turn my home into a flipping chip-shop will you?" He lunged at Aspern, only to be deflected by his lanky son.

"That's why you wanted all those odd bits of property," Jan stated. "I had a very informative chat with Mr. Dawson as we were driving to the police station."

"It's my land," whined Aspern. "I can rent it out to Bonnie Burgers if I like."

"Well, you're not getting this place," Susi declared. "We spent the night together, and that's that."

The solicitor concurred. "I believe, Lord Aspern, that you may have to call off the deal. The Bonnie Burger Corporation cannot possibly fulfill the terms of the peppercorn rent as stated in this document." He tapped the computer printout of the medieval deed.

"And I so wanted to live in the South of France," moaned Aspern.

"Do you have to rent out all your properties to Bonnie Burgers?" Susi asked. The odious lecher of last night had become a frightened little man in a suit far too youthful for him.

"I suppose I could explain that this one has...sentimental value," Aspern said. He straightened his shoulders. "They'll just have to be satisfied with twenty Bonnie Burgers in London instead of twenty-one." He turned to Susi. "I wish you would tell me how you did it," he said, with an avaricious grin. "I could arrange a tour, with Lime Green Jello. We would make a fortune!"

"It's a monthly thing," Susi said. "Really."

Aspern blinked. Then he glanced about the shabby room, shrugged, and marched to the door, his solicitor right behind him. At the front door he turned.

"Next year," he announced, "Next year...The rent's been raised to fifty pounds!"

Back at the Dorchester, properly suited, shaved, and scented, Lord Aspern rose to greet the Chief Executive Officer of Bonnie Burgers, Jeffrey Jellicoe, Jr.

Mr. Jellicoe was a tall, slender young man, with long fair hair pulled back into a neat ponytail, dressed in the latest in Italian relaxed suit in ice-cream colors. Aspern blinked at the sight and suddenly put the face back into its latest context.

"Mr. Jellicoe?" he quavered.

Lime Green Jello grinned back. "We just keep running into each other, don't we, Aspern? Now, what's this I hear about one piece of property that isn't in the deal?'

"Sit down, my boy, and let me explain," Aspern said, a gleam of hope rising in his eyes. "It seems there is a thing called a Peppercorn Rent...."

Rats, Wrong Alley
by Tim Johnson

When Snakes heard an angry knock at midnight, he knew it wasn't good.

The humming neon sign outside cast a pink glow into the dim room. Snakes was sitting on a ratty couch, sipping a warm beer and trying to watch whatever station would come in on the antiquated television. Oscar was sitting at the table, playing a game of solitaire with greasy cards, and humming stupidly.

Snakes put the beer on the floor and crossed the musty room; stepping over a barrage of trash — empty beer cans and liquor bottles, old pizza boxes, filthy clothes. When he reached the door, he peered through the peephole and nearly shit himself. He saw Mikey Gabrieli standing in the hallway, red-faced and pounding on the door with the handle of the gun.

"Snakes, you open this fucking door or I swear to God I'll shoot the lock and come blow your fucking balls off."

"Hang on," Snakes said, his hand trembling as he reached for the lock.

"Who the hell is that?" Oscar asked, looking up with the same dopey look glued to his pudgy face. Snakes ignored Oscar and unlocked the door. Before he could turn the knob, Mikey Gabrieli forced his way in with the gun in the air, business-end first. "All right, Snakes," he said, shoving the gun in Snakes' face, "you've had enough time. Where's my fucking money?"

"Oh shit," Oscar yelped, jumping to his feet.

"You stay there," Mikey barked, turning the gun on Oscar. Oscar nodded and put his hands in the air.

"Now," Mikey returned the gun to Snakes, "my money."

"Okay," Snakes said, "let me get it."

"Fine."

Snakes scampered across the littered studio to the kitchenette. He passed Oscar—still frozen like a sweating ice sculpture—and opened a cabinet. He reached into the back, pulled out a dusty jar, and removed a wad of cash.

"Bring it here," Mikey demanded, waving the gun.

Snakes did as he was told. Mikey grabbed the money and counted it. He shoved the gun against Snakes' head. "This is only six hundred. I gave you a grand's worth of dope to sell. I think your fucking brains splattered on that wall is worth about four-hundred. What'd you think, fat shit?"

Oscar said nothing; simply stared with wide eyes.

"Please," Snakes pleaded. "The landlord caught me with a bunch of cash, and I'm backed up on rent. If I didn't pay him, he would've thrown me out." Snakes swallowed hard. His mouth felt like charcoal. "I'll get you the money, I swear it."

Mikey's eyes were hard.

"Okay. I'll give you till noon tomorrow to get that cash. I don't give a fuck how you get it, but I want it. And if not," his free hand jerked forward and grabbed Snakes by the balls; he pressed the gun to Snakes neck and leaned in, "I *will* blow your fucking brains out the back of your skull. You dig?"

"Yeah," Snakes struggled to say. "Sure thing, Mikey."

"Good. Very good." He started toward the door. "And don't you run off on me. Because if you do, and I find you—and I will—I swear I'll tear your heart out through your ass."

Snakes nodded his agreement, gritting his teeth to fight the pain.

"I don't fucking get it," Mikey said with a smirk, "how're you suppose to get any money from selling if you can't pay me for what I give you? You assholes ain't smoking all that shit, are you?"

Snakes and Oscar remained silent. Mikey slammed the door. Snakes stumbled to the couch, moaning and rubbing himself.

"*Fuck!*" he shouted. "Oscar, you asshole!"

The story about the landlord had been a lie. In fact, Snakes and Oscar had made a decent profit. However, after a big sale, Oscar went out to get shit-faced, picked up a cheap hooker and passed out. When he came to, the hooker was gone with all the money.

"Shit, Snakes," Oscar said, "I'm sorry, man."

"Well sorry ain't gonna keep a bullet outta my head. Just what the fuck am I gonna do? Because it's me that's in deep shit for this fuck-up. *Your* fuck-up. I swear, Oscar, sometimes I could fucking kill you." He leaned back and grunted. "Shit, I feel like my nuts got run over by a taxi."

Oscar chuckled. Then he stood for a moment in quiet thought.

"Snakes?" Oscar said after a minute.

"What is it?"

"I think I know how we can get that money."

"Run this by me one more time."

Only an hour had passed since the ball-busting confrontation with Mikey Gabrieli. Snakes and Oscar were walking along a bleak street, in search of quick cash. Oscar was hiding a gun in his hooded sweatshirt. Snakes had stuffed his gun into the front of his pants.

"Okay," Oscar said. "There's a shitty little store on River Street, a twenty-four-hour place. I've been in there a few times real late at night. Or real early in the morning, however you look at it. Anyhow, the guy there is some dumb shit. I swear I've stolen liquor from that place a dozen times. Just slip a bottle in my jacket and slip out. The dumb clerk never says a single word."

"But we're not talking about emptying a cheap liquor bottle. We're talking about emptying the register. This is *armed robbery* here. Some big shit. I could go back to prison for this."

"Relax, Snakes," Oscar said. "We'll go in, take all the cash from the register, and be out and away before that fucking clerk knows what happened." Oscar removed two ski masks from a small duffel bag hooked over his shoulder. He handed Snakes a mask and slid the other on his head.

"Yeah, but what if the guy only has…say, forty bucks in the register. Then what?"

"Ah," Oscar said with a smirk, "that's the best part. You see, real early in the morning, like around five, someone comes and collects the money. I seen them do it once. They come and clean out the register. The whole earnings from the day before. And I swear there was at least four-hundred there. *At least.*"

They continued to walk through the slummy neighborhood. Oscar glanced up at a tall, rundown building.

"Hey. I know that place. You hear the story about that dump?"

"No," Snakes responded; he hadn't heard the story and he didn't want to. He needed to stay focused.

"I used to have a buddy that lived there," Oscar began. "Sold him his dope. While back. Then the place got condemned. Rat problem. Suckers were chewing up the wood and tearing the place apart. So then later, when the weather'd get cold, bunch of bums would shack up in there. Suppose they didn't mind sharing the place with a bunch of filthy rats."

Snakes looked up at the old building. Nothing about it looked warm. It looked cold and ugly and bad.

"Eventually," Oscar continued, "the cops bust in there to kick all the winos out. But when they get inside, they find all the bums dead."

"Froze to death?" Snakes offered. He was remembering how Oscar had gotten him in this mess.

"Nah. They found the bums dead with big-ass bite marks in 'em. Chewed to shit. Kinda funny. I'm sure some of them bums ate a rat or two in their desperate days. What a kick in the nuts — the rats eating *them*. I heard the little bastards made these weird nests in the bodies."

"Rats ate them?" Snakes asked doubtfully. Oscar looked over his shoulder at the building. The convenience store on River Street came into view.

"Shit, I don't know. Just what I heard. You ever hear about that government lab in one of the burbs? Some guy told me that Uncle Sam's been doing some pretty fucking weird tests up there. Working with plasma-lasers and plutonium and shit. Stuff so goddamn hot it can burn a bitchin' hole right through reality. Now, suppose those boys dumped some spooky shit in the river? It runs through the city. You know how the rats crawl their dirty asses up here from the river. Hell, maybe —"

"Look," Snakes interrupted, very agitated, anxious, "I really don't give a flying fuck about some bullshit story you heard from a doped-up crackhead. I just want to do this, get that cash, and live to suffer another day. Got it?"

"Yeah. Sure thing."

The two stood across the street from the targeted store. Snakes took a deep breath.

"All right. Nice and smooth and easy."

But that was not how it went.

*　　　*　　　*

They burst out of the convenience store like a cork from a cheap liquor bottle. As they stumbled to the empty street, the store window exploded. Glass rained onto the littered storefront.

"Come on, come on! Move your ass, man!" Snakes shouted to Oscar.

Once again Oscar fucked up. Oscar had sneaked a peek at a nudie mag, lowered his gun just long enough for the clerk to react. If they didn't hide somewhere soon, they'd get caught. Snakes knew damn well that with his past record they'd be more than happy to toss his ass back in the joint.

Oscar pumped his portly legs, trailing behind. He nearly fell crossing over the streetcar tracks. The two bolted down the dilapidated sidewalk, trying to escape the accusing glow of overhead streetlights. When they came to a lightless opening, Snakes cut to the right into the masking darkness of a deep, narrow alley. Oscar followed. The dour stench of grease and trash hung in the air like burning rubber.

"Shit, Oscar," Snakes complained, leaning against a sooty brick wall. He pulled off his ski mask. "You never said anything about that clerk having a gun. What the fuck was that?"

Oscar yanked off his mask and tucked it under his arm. He shoved his gun back into the front pocket of his sweatshirt and leaned forward, palms on his knees. "Sorry, man. How was I supposed to know he'd have a gun?"

"You're always sorry," Snakes barked. "Now I'm totally fucked. Mikey Gabrieli wants me dead, we almost got our heads blown off, any minute now the pigs are gonna to be after us, I'll probably go back to prison—if not, I'll be killed. And you're *sorry*. Well that's just fucking great!"

Oscar looked away. Then he peered through the darkness at one of the rundown buildings bordering the alley.

"Hey," he said offhandedly, "that's the building we passed on the way over here. The one I was telling you about. I wonder if there's still rats in — "

"Shut up!"

The expected sound of police sirens drifted from a distance, like smoke spreading from dry brush.

"Oh shit," Oscar mumbled, still gawking at the crummy building. Then he looked away and started toward the street.

"No." Snakes reached out and pulled Oscar back. "We can't go back out in the street. If we're in the light, they might see us."

Oscar gazed into the darkness of the alley. "There," he said, and pointed at a forgotten dumpster. "We can hide in there."

"I don't know," Snakes said. "They'd probably look in there."

"Well then what? What the hell are we going to do?" Fear trickled into Oscar's voice like water into a sinking boat.

Snakes opened his mouth to reply, then stopped. Something caught his eye. It was a lump, resting against the wall further into the alley.

"What's that?" he asked, pointing at the lump.

"Shit, I don't know. It's probably just a fucking bum."

An idea burst in Snakes mind like a firecracker, shedding light on a possible escape route. A real dirty one.

"Come on," he told Oscar. Oscar followed Snakes timidly, deeper into the alley. The darkness was so thick that Snakes couldn't be sure if the lump was actually a

person. It could have been a bag of garbage. Smelled like
it. But as his eyes adjusted, he realized that it *was* a person.

"Snakes," Oscar asked restlessly, "what the hell are
we doing?"

Staring at the bum — just a lump — Snakes saw his
plan rapidly unwinding in his mind, setting him free. He
adjusted the gun.

"Perfect," he said. "He's out cold — drunk. Shoot
him."

"*What?*" Oscar asked.

"*Kill him.* Now. Trust me."

"Snakes, man, why the hell would I — ?"

The sirens were louder.

"*Just fucking do it!*"

"Shit," Oscar moaned, oblivious. Fueled by
confusion, he aimed his gun at the still body and fired. The
report resonated throughout the alley. The body twitched
and remained still.

"Good," Snakes said, wetting his dry lips. "Now,
Oscar, put on your ski mask."

Oscar sighed, did as he was told. Adjusting the
mask on his face, Oscar found himself staring down the
barrel of a gun.

"Snakes, man, what the hell — ?"

Snakes fired. A bullet tore through Oscar's throat.
A spatter of crimson slime spewed out the back of his neck.
He dropped to the greasy pavement like a hefty pile of shit.

The sound of sirens died. Snakes turned and looked
towards the desolate city street and saw blue flashes
brushing gently against the buildings. He knew he had to
move quickly.

He placed his gun in the hand of the dead homeless
man. When he tilted back the cadaver's head to slip on his
ski mask, Snakes staggered back, covered his mouth to
keep from puking, took a deep breath and leaned in for a

closer look. Oscar hadn't murdered the lump. The bum's neck had been torn open. Deep scratches surrounded the grotesque, red-black hole that reminded Snakes of a dog scratching at a door, wanting to get out, or wanting to get in.

Snakes averted his horrified stare. The cruisers were so close now that he could actually hear tires slowly passing over the sandy streets. The cops were sure to look in the alley any second. Snakes cursorily shoved his mask over the bum's dead face, careful not to touch the wound. Then he turned and bolted toward the old dumpster. He stepped over Oscar's body.

"Sorry, man" he said, remembering all the times Oscar fucked up. He reached the dumpster, lifted the lid, jumped in head-first and let the top fall down. There was a small rusted hole in the front. Snakes peered through. He watched as a police cruiser slowly approached, shining a searchlight. The car slowed, pulled toward the alley, then stopped. Two officers stepped out of the cruiser, one directed the light, the other held out a gun.

"Police," one said, "sit up on your knees and put your hands behind your head."

Snakes almost laughed, but something rustled in the garbage beneath him.

"Nick," the cop with the light said to his partner, "I don't think those boys'll be doing much of anything."

Nick approached the two bodies. "I guess not," he said, tucking the gun back in its holster. He removed the radio from his belt. "Yeah," he said into the receiver, "we found the two…No, no, it's under control—in a manner of speaking…Uh huh…Well, these guys are about as dead as a couple of fish in a frying pan…Who the hell knows…Yeah, no rush."

He hooked the radio back on his belt and removed a flashlight.

In the dumpster, trash trembled beneath Snakes; something was breathing faintly through all the reeking rubbish, just below him. It sounded almost like a panting dog. He wanted to move, to get away from whatever the hell was working its way through the rotten garbage.

"You hear something?" the cop with the searchlight asked, shining the light on the dumpster.

Snakes jerked his head away from the rusted peephole.

"Eh," Nick said, "just rats in the garbage."

Relief washed over Snakes. But as he felt something brush against his leg—something that felt *much* bigger than any rat he'd ever seen—his heart lapsed into double-time.

"Speak of the devil," Nick said, casting light on the dead bum. He pulled back the ski mask and looked at the torn, reddened flesh.

"Hey, O'Malley," he said to his partner, "come get a look at this."

Snakes watched as O'Malley approached the bloody mess.

"I don't see how this fellow could have tried to hold up that shop down the road. From the look of this, I'd say he's been dead for a few days."

"So what'd you think—?"

The crawling creature beneath Snakes' legs shuffled toward his crotch. Both cops turned and stared at the dumpster. Snakes pissed his pants. But not because he was afraid of being caught; that fear—along with the fear of Mikey Gabrieli, or prison, or anything else—faded to second stage. The creature between his legs took center stage. He could feel its hot breath through his wet pants. *Plenty of dark corners in the world – places where all kinds of fucked up things can hide and seek.*

Through the rusted hole, he saw the two cops step over Oscar's body. Snakes pulled his head back. Total blackness.

A single image filled the space before his mind's eye. He saw the raw hamburger of the bum's throat. Something was looking for a bite to eat. A place to nest.

What the hell could have done that? Snakes wondered, and started to scramble back.

But it was too late.

Suddenly, with a noise like a snapping mousetrap, fiery pain exploded in his groin and shot through his entire body. He felt razor sharp, needle teeth digging deep into his crotch, chomping forcefully — up and down, up and down. Snakes groped helplessly between his twitching legs, trying to fight the little beast, trying to wrestle it away. When his jittering hands grasped the slimy, coarse hairs on the thing's body — easily the size of a cat — Snakes knew it was too late; he could feel the thing's furious head *inside* him, clearing a path. As terror and agony surged through him, he looked down and caught a glimpse of something that didn't look like a rat at all.

Stuff so goddamn hot it can burn a bitchin' hole right through reality.

He stopped screaming, and coldness danced over him, holding the hand of darkness.

*   *   *

The dumpster lid crashed open. Lights reached into the gruesome darkness. Nick and O'Malley peered over the edge just in time to see a thick, pink-gray tail slither like a snake into the bleeding tear as the anomaly burrowed itself deep inside the dead man.

"Well suck me on a Saturday," Nick said. "Did you see that little bastard go?"

O'Malley nodded and let the dumpster lid slam shut. "*He* won't be cold when the winter months roll around."

"Yeah," Nick said with a chuckle. "Plenty to eat, too." He looked up at the decrepit, abandoned buildings. "Well, it was slinking in that dumpster, waiting to eat some garbage. The way I figure, it got what it wanted." He paused for a moment and inhaled a whiff of the sour city air. "One less criminal on the streets, one less cell to fill."

"Say," O'Malley said to his partner, looking at Oscar with a famished look in his beady eyes, "you hungry?"

"Yes, indeed," Nick answered, licking his lips. He neared the bleeding cadaver, grinning with protruding buckteeth. The two officers hauled Oscar's body away, their pink-gray tails shivering excitedly beneath tidy uniforms.

Brilliant Suspension
by Trina Shealy Orton

Nameless and faceless, just a piece of meat, the man hung above a knife-sharp rocky pit. Time had stopped. When he found consciousness the first time, he had thought he still might break free but quickly surrendered hope. Opened or closed, his traitor eyes swallowed stygian night. He didn't care. He was and was not. He floated and sank.

Water trickled over distant stone. At first, he would imagine anything to soothe his misery - cool breezes flowing over his bare flesh or water to moisten his cracked lips - but the images became torture. He gave up replaying his life. He forgot the things he should have said to make things right.

Things scrambled in the dark under him. Their noises ricocheted in a dance of expectation. When he'd still been producing bodily waste, he heard them consuming it, and the greedy slurping sounds crashed into the crevices to grate cruelly in his ears.

He was purified of everything, including his last supper (alcohol and nicotine), and waiting. He did not know what would happen after he died and couldn't resent those who had done this to him. If they reappeared, he might even thank them for his newfound clarity. He didn't bother to wonder where they had gone after blind-siding him outside the bar. He would never know the owner of the voice that lured him into the alley.

He'd been tipping back a few at the local bar's happy hour. It was something he did to relax after work and to dull his bitterness. Since Lora had left him, he'd been so lonely. Desperation and need had made him follow the voice's beckoning when it had said his name; it had been the call of a siren.

They'd carried him to this place and stripped him, tying him up like a pig bound for the spit and leaving him suspended in the chilly dark for days that bled into each other.

He couldn't remember the last time he'd seen light; he'd been unconscious when they'd left him, taking their torches away. The stink of pitch had filled his nostrils for ages.

He felt his bones creaking, slowly breaking through his shoulder and hip. His flesh was sloughing off in large portions from his arms and legs, his face and torso. Long, black hair had once covered his head. In spite of all this, he did not worry.

Giddiness rose inside him, surprising him with its intensity. He tried to laugh, but after so long in silence, even those gravelly barks deafened him. His eardrums burst and oozed bright ichor, but he couldn't stop. His laughter became so loud that the air reverberated. The rocks began to vibrate, and smaller stones clattered downward. Eerie echoes bounced off the walls and back. A haunting symphony and a gout of rust-colored blood sprang from his lips.

The shifting crevices shook free the hooks that held his ropes, and he fell quickly. The shock of his limbs flopping and his skeletal fingers failing to find purchase silenced him. He waited for the impact.

Inches before impaling himself on the rocks of the pit, light began to seep through his skin in bursts of energy that grew brighter, pushing him back up. He levitated. He could see his surroundings, a tiny man-made cavern, before his eyes were incinerated.

His luminescence turned his body white-hot. The last of his flesh blasted clear of bone and exposed muscle that became ragged strips before melting away. His viscera and blood rained down to coat the scrambling things.

And then - Oblivion.

When consciousness returned a lifetime later, he rediscovered his eyes. A soft light barely made its way to the walls, but he could see that he was still inside the cavern. Rather than being bound like before, he now floated feet-first over the abyss. His own body provided the illumination.

Slowly he lifted a hand, experiencing no pain even after his long confinement. His body was again flesh, but instead of his usual solid mocha, he was a perfect golden translucence threaded with pale blue strands. The strands moved when he wiggled his fingers. Verdigris blue currents flashed up and down his limbs at regular intervals.

He figured it was a dying illusion. The breeze caressed his thighs when there had been no breeze, his lost hair now tickled the small of his back, and the once dry tongue now moist... all figments of his imagination, a desire to make Will be Truth.

He ran a hand over his chest, shivering at the freedom. He closed his eyes and threw his head back, hair rustling, and began to take one step forward...

A muffled whisper of sound brought him back to reality. With a snap of his head, he sought the source of disturbance. He saw Them waiting before him and knew this was no dream. He was new flesh. One stepped forward, a vaguely familiar female avatar. She was like him but gifted with silver flesh. Wispy, tattered wings floated absently out from her back.

The others in the waiting cluster presented a variety of different colors. All had the same fragile-looking wings as her.

    With a start, he noticed his own wings. He idly
thought of wrapping them around himself, and they
fluttered forward gently in compliance. He accepted that
he'd been hand-picked.

    "Welcome," the female said, in a hushed voice.
Something clicked in his brain at the sound. The smile
playing about on her lips teased him. She opened her
opalescent arms to him, and he recognized why she was so
familiar. Hers was the voice in the alley.

    "Welcome home Chan."

Blue Elephants
by Jenifer Jourdanne

Parrots

One of the reasons I love L.A. - you're driving down Santa Monica Blvd and it's just lovely, little old women taking their tiny dogs out for walks, gay men coming home from the gym, people in cafes lounging about...and then, bam, you cross onto the wrong side and it's like that school where Joe Clark had to bring his megaphone. I like that. If I had kids I would drop them off there and tell them to go play Charlie's Angels.

But I don't have kids, so instead: **Parrot Prison**

What else can I legally lock up if it misbehaves without someone making me out to be Mommy Dearest? Her cage is huge. It has more toys in it than the playpen of a infertile couple's adopted Romanian baby. Yet, she spends no time in this cage except for sleeping. I am not very good at setting rules. I am a pushover parrot mother. I cook her food and she has multiple play gyms. I even attended a fairplex bird show, aptly named The Bird Mart, to find new toys. Yes, that is the sad individual I have become. That person you see in pet stores reading the content label of bird food? Hi, that's me now. I am 3 aisles away from buying wild bird seed in a housedress. Perhaps this is why I do not have children. If I did, you would find me with 30 kids, making them dinner, coaching their soccer games -- I would forget who I was and then you'd find me and a cart living on Santa Monica Blvd, while John Walsh profiles a lost woman accused of putting her children in an unused parrot cage and running off with a guy from Chuck E Cheese who was found in a hotel beat with a Blahnik heel, circa Spring 2002.

I have actually dragged friends to The Bird Mart. This is how you know you have good friends; if they will accompany you to a hobby, pet or computer show. I went to a computer show once. A man waved and screamed **HEY YOU** and I had visions of some man I told to fuck off in an IM coming to get me, because I suffer from hubris. He probably just wanted to sell me something. I can admit that now.

Bird Shows are very scary. Imagine Star Trek people with birds. For one day they traded in their pointy ears for bird jewelry and airbrushed bird shirts. I love my parrot, but I do not love the Bird Mart. I don't love anything that ends in Mart. You can never expect anything good from such a place. First, you have to park too far away. I had to ride a tram that said on the top EVERYBODYS BIRDMART. I felt like I was in the Doo-Daa Parade and as the tram crossed the real street on the way to the sad bird mart, we all said in unison, **"I hope no one we know sees us!"**

Once inside, I spent 10 hours talking to a man about feeding your bird LIVE SPROUTS. He was worse than the Juiceman. I now sprout her extra food every morning because I am scared of him. He lectured me about the importance of live sprouts or my bird would die an early death. He stood there jumping around and shouting *"BUT BIRDS SEE, THEY NEED LIVING FOOD TO SURVIVE!!"*. So I make them and she hates them. If she could talk, she would have said: **"Where are my strawberries you bitch?"**

Next to him were two women who sew and sell Cozy Hut Tents for your bird to sleep in. What an untapped gold mine venture. Anyone who can be told a bird will sleep in one of these things at night like a good little camper is as naive....as me. I was walking by laughing at the American Flag and Peter Rabbit print tents; then I saw a leopard print one and became one of those dorks who own a bird cozy hut tent. I like to think since I was raised in a cult that I am easily brainwashed. At first I thought it was a fine idea, I mean who wants to sleep on a perch? Don't your feet hurt? When I showed it to my parrot, if she could talk yet, I assure you she was saying **"Hey moron, I perch to sleep, what the hell were you thinking? Wait a minute. Were you at the bird show? So my new owner is a dork, this is fabulous."** My bird thought I was trying to send her home to Jesus. Those were some smart sewing women. They even had a photo album full of people's birds who just loved their cozy huts. I know damn well now that everyone put super glue on their birds feet in order to obtain photographs of a bird anywhere *near* a bird cozy hut.

I also went to Babies R Us and bought her baby toys she can push the buttons on for stimulation. So in the morning she gets bored waiting for us to talk to her and she starts pushing them and from the next room you hear GREEN BUG. YELLOW DUCK. PEEKABOO. I saw a lot of people buying baby clothes in Babies R US because that is what you are supposed to do there, not shop for your bird. I pity Babies R Us if I ever get a monkey. My sister was buying baby clothes there, and I said *"Yea, they're cute and then someone sticks them on a baby and ruins them!"* Did you know there are crickets in Babies R Us?

In L.A. this pet mania goes one step further. I was at the vet a few months back when a man came in with his dog. He was old hippie guy with a tie-dyed shirt. His dog had cancer and they discussed how the dog developed cancer because he internalized all his anger from his divorce. His chakras were blocked and his aura was cloudy. So between the chemo and the group visualization, they have things under control. And the others are nodding and saying "I have heard this works wonders. I have books about it." A woman got up and hugged him. He was trying

to visualize white healing light for my pet. I wonder if that
happens in Iowa or Alabama.

*I now have one monstrous cage outfitted with all a bird
wants but a bird that never uses it. So if any of you live in L.A.,
have misbehaving children and a dream to detain your rotten
kids, let me know. I will remove all the toys and we can play
JAIL. I am sure someone has an extra prison uniform, although I
prefer those old striped versions to the new day-glo orange
pantsuits. It's that little hat at the top of the striped versions that
does it for me. It's very Hamburglar. Then we can release them in
L.A. and hunt them down with a helicopter.*

The Single Persons Seat
or *I ain't bringin in the dishes*

Perceptions are based upon my own family, please
ignore me because your own group of family may not be
this retarded. You yourself may have changed the course of
married person history when you refused to clear a plate.
God bless you.

Bless the men who clear plates and bless the women
who refuse to pick them up. Bless those Greek people who
break them under their feet when they dance. I would bless
the Jewish people, but basically you only break one glass
and it's at a wedding and we are not going to applaud the
fact you step on glass, unless you do it without the aid of
shoes or socks in which case....I am going to call Ripley's
or The Jim Rose Freak Circus because you may have
abilities he could use.

I have figured out why married people get gifts. But
really, what do single people get? Nothing. We don't get a

party. We should though, do you people have any idea
how much we saved you?

- engagement party
- wedding shower
- wedding present
- the baby shower
- birth of said baby
- anniversary

Damn it, you owe us like $2000 in cash. Not to
mention the food we save you when we come over with
one tiny friend or a guy who refuses to eat your cooking.
Okay, so he or she did drink all your alcohol, but comp us
dammit, we're single.

And we screw up your seating arrangement. We
love that. Sometimes we bring three people just to mess
with your heads. Screw up your napkin rings - don't look
now - the single person stole your napkin ring. We know
your trick, you try to put us in that one extra chair like in a
bad scene from the Peter Sellers movie *The Party*. This chair
is a foot smaller or has a wobbly leg. You even try to put us
closest to the door, or in a corner like Domino's family. But
they only put her there because she is the only one who
fits. It's a really tiny corner. You can't even see her from the
end of the table; just the top of her head like a Peanuts
character or a platinum Chia pet.

We also tell your kids the truth about everything
when you sit us too close to the kiddy table. This is why
they hate you after dinner. I have found that conversation,
although cramped for the legs, is much better at the kiddy
table. If this got out, there would be no one left at the adult
table. You cannot compete with "I saw a 2 hundred pound
caterpillar eating a kid in my yard" All you have is "So, it
looks like rain tonight Bob.' You all suck. You are no

Algonquin Round Table. Your kids are over there talking about world politics.

Kid: "Hey, this kid at school is named Ashley so we beat him up"

Me: "Why?"

Kid looking at me like I am a complete moron: "Because his name is Ashley and he's a BOY."

Somewhere at a table across town you can be sure, Ashley's mom is clearing plates.

The kids' table is equal opportunity. Where else can you be 5'9" and drive, yet have a kid ask you "so what grade are you in?"

"5th....I'm in 5th, it's such a bitch." You say with a straight face. This is followed by sympathetic nodding from real life 5th graders.

The mothers and wives at these parties - who clear the tables and then retire to the kitchen to do the dishes and leave the men "out there talking." - who are these women and why do I wish their heads would explode? Women like that are the reason I hate having my hair done. Stepford Wife Pod People. All sitting around dreaming about the plates. God help me if I ever get up and clear plates with you. When does this hit you? It's like being 12 and wondering when you are going to get your period, Oh my god, is it going to happen when I am wearing white pants? Wrap a sweater around your waist and no one will notice.

I am not saying that all married women or any sort of women are like this. I have many times picked up a boyfriends plate, but never because I felt part of the female "Hi we represent the Plate Picker Uppers League" population. Screw you. I would just leave his plate sitting there to make a point. But here is what I have witnessed in certain household parties. When you bring a boyfriend, they don't expect you to clear plates. It's like the wedding ceremony has it in the fine print: "You will be expected to clear tables." Maybe this is why married people get gifts. They are paying you for the services you will perform in the future.

But if you witness the clearing of the plates, you have to see it's a finely executed ballet choreography. Or water aerobics. It's like the wave.. but longer. It starts with one woman. She gets up to clear her husband's plates, and if by cue, the next wife sees her and she is up, followed by the next. She doesn't want to seem like she didn't think of it first. But for the men, it's a spy move. They very carefully look at one another and then perform an almost imperceptible head gesture that is too fast for the human eye to catch to tell the other men to run, run for the living room. This is followed by each man escaping in sync to his wife lifting his plate. Lift. Look. Run. The men are very quiet as they do this. Go ahead, be very loud. They won't ask you to help because they are married and it was in a clause in their vow.

Now I suppose some man is going to tell me that he helps clear the plates. If you do, you are a sucker, get out while you can.

Divorced women....they are still married when it comes to clearing plates. They automatically jump up. The only divorced woman who doesn't clear plates is Liz Taylor. Children who want to clear plates are clearly pod people in the making but you can't clear plates because your parents will scream "WHAT ARE YOU, CRAZY!? YOU'RE GOING TO DROP THAT!" Unless your family has a caterer in which case, the pod women *still* jump up and down to oversee the plate clearers because....they have to do something, you bought them a hutch to hold all those plates.

So I sat there. What was I supposed to do? Stand? Sit? Clear? Escape? I am lost in a sea of people who understand what is expected. But then again, I was thrown out of my niece's Barbie hotel last week. She had security escort my dolls out. So it's not like I am one with the pod.

I have options. I can go in the kitchen and pretend I am one of them, but clearly I am not. I still stumble drunkenly into clubs and Hustler and these women are talking about hysterectomies and nipple chafing. Eww run. These are the very monsters who order huge plates of food and then say "I will have a diet coke, tee hee." We are not amused. I swear to god, at moments like this near my family, I am amazed these Stepford Pod Women get sex at all. I really am. It's a whole room of Special Hair Barbies. Live in person. On ice. With Happy Family Volvos.

I am clearly not cool with the kids any longer because I cannot fit in an Ikea tube to the playhouse. So it's old people or the men. Old people, there's a no. It's totally YaYa Sisterhood over there. Run before they send you to the store for Depends undergarments.

If you go to the men they will think you want them. My friend Skin once told me this and I never believed him. I do now, Skin. I really do. One husband of a friend told me it was the way I said "fine and how are you." He said I clearly was saying "I want you." He had a Magnum PI mustache but the handlebar version. No PT Barnum, I did not want you. Wow, no one told me I had that effect. I totally missed my calling as a phone sex operator. Maybe it is because I am laid back and do not have that look on my face like their wife that screams "WHERE ARE THE KIDS NOW?" It's okay, their wives are thinking you want their husbands too. My sister told me that her own friends thought I wanted their husbands. Most of them look like ABC sitcom dads. Guys, who are you kidding? You people had to do the Lift-Look-Run to get into this room. No one wants you. You have been trained. Do you realize the amount of retraining it would take if we did want you?

You have been minivaned and taught how to mow the lawn to drown out your wife's bitching. It's all downhill from here. No, we want you right now for one reason. The men's area of the house is where all the uncomplicated talk without the bitch factor is. Bob is not over here asking Dan if he likes his new hairdo. John is not asking Tom if his ass looks large in those trousers.

For instance, the women are in that room over there saying: "That Mary, do you know what she did to me," followed by widened eyes and all the other women gathering around for a story with a hushed "NO, WHAT?!" question.

Not you men. You would just say: "Hey Brad, that Mary….she's a slut."

This is followed by much nodding and one of the men, usually the one with the most hair, he says "DON'T I KNOW IT" like he personally knows. He gets a high five from another guy and then he hands you a cigar.

Note: If you have gay men in your family this could be a very different scenario. The bitch factor will be coming from their area as well. But it will be better groomed, more sarcastic and highly amusing.

The evasion of the clearing of the plates does not work if you are married, yet at the dinner party without spouse. They know you're married; start clearing old people's plates. Either old people or the kids. We bought you a blender; we could care less if you are solo. Start clearing.

Single people are not even expected to clear their own plate. In the history of family or friends parties, I have never taken my plate or a boyfriends plate. It is scooped up quickly, very Sim like, by a wife without her spouse or an old lady.

Could you avoid this forever? Yes I believe you can. I believe in a world where you can be any person and

decide if you want to clear your plate. You do have
options. You can try something no one has ever done. Place
the plate on an already growing stack of married lifter's
plates. She will think you were helping, so beware. They
may invite you into the kitchen and you will never escape.
You will come out hours later with five years sucked out of
your life expectancy and you'll have a wrinkle and know
all the horrors of natural childbirth. The plus side is that
they may have tranquilizers back there.

You could perform a reverse whammy on them and
have your boyfriend take your plate, make it a first. But
then the other men will never let him into the plateless
male escape group. They will think he's gay and your
boyfriend will never go for it. If he is foreign, just tell him it
is the custom here for men to take their own damn plate in.
Or you can do the Auntie Mame thing and hire a personal
sherpa plate lifter guy, or pay a kid 5 dollars. This will be
seen as stuck up and they will not invite you to the kitchen
(a plus) but the men may steal your five dollar trick, but
they will never get away with it because they would be
forced to use their own kid and never pay up and the kid
will be on to their game. You can make an old person do it,
but God will look down on you.

There are no easy answers. Hire servants.

Blue Elephants

America is in a big bubble but you can play small
world all day long without ever having to leave its borders.
Yes. You can. Last week I was with Domino while she did
some scary executive things. Really I went for the Little
Meeting Big Lunch thing. After, she had to give a demo to
young girls in middle school about glamour. The boys
volunteered her because they were too scared. It's like

Courtney Love teaching your kids Sex Ed. Good luck because I was going along for the ride.

LA was still under the impression of summer; it was a bazillion degrees, which is what I get for living in a colonized desert, but I don't care what anyone says - I like it. We had crazy people running for governor; I am never leaving now. We headed to an area in Downtown Disney which...is a lot of tourist stores in an outdoor setting with one very very important thing – it's outdoors. So no air conditioning unless you're the bubble boy. Downtown Disney did not inform me. If Walt can freeze his head then the very least he can do is air condition Downtown Disney.

Now there were only a few restaurants but one of them was THE RAINFOREST CAFÉ. Kids were leaving it crying, so that was where I went. It's like a real Disney environment right in a restaurant. You walk in and you have to speak to the big plastic blue elephant. They actually say from their little headphones "**APPROACH THE BLUE ELEPHANT!**", and something blasts you with cool air. I bet its Disney cootie disinfectant. I bet Walt had that whole Howard Hughes germ disorder. Never in my life had I wished more that I was on LSD.

So you approach the blue elephant and THERE ARE PEOPLE IN IT, they are *in* the blue elephant, wearing hats and microphones and I said to Dom "*I can't believe we are here, this is so wrong, do they serve alcohol?*" And apparently Walt does think of everything, because there is alcohol.

All of the sudden the whole restaurant shakes and goes dark and thunder breaks out and lightening flashes and the jungle noises start and the animated animals start moving. And the little kids start crying. I say "**AM I HAVING A PANIC ATTACK?**" and she says "*No it's supposed to be a rainforest!*" which would explain its name. Wow, that is so fucked up. People bring their kids here to scare them; I love this place. Forget you; I am moving into the Rainforest Café.

And when it is time they call your name and say: *"Domino party of two, your adventure awaits you, approach the blue elephant and please await your safari."* If you don't show up they say: **Bob, party of 12, Bob Party of 12, your safari has left without you.** Yea, screw you Bob, you are not going to be seeing any fake rainforest today.

While drinking margaritas, we relished the moments when the fake storms came and the lights went out and the kids cried and screamed because life sized animatronic gorillas and elephants were coming to kill them. This is how life should be.

So here is my review of the Rainforest Café.

Pros

- It's dark
- Scares the hell out of kids
- Has alcohol
- Cute men in safari suits
- Makes children cry
- You get to watch children - those scared children cry
- If your kids are bad, you can go there and sit next to the gorillas and watch them cry

Cons

- If your kids are good, you take them there as a treat and they still cry.
- Although the bar is called The Magic Mushroom, they have no mushrooms just like the Opium Den has no opium. False advertising is not my friend.

- Disney people ride the monorail to this place; it's fanny pack heaven. Casual clothes are not my friend.
- Kids are allowed, but without them, you would have no one to laugh at.
- The alcohol is not strong enough
- The food has dorky names and you have to repeat them "*I'll have the Monkeylicious Safari Salad on Elephant Ear Bread*" you can't appear sophisticated ordering that, you just can't. (Can be seen as a pro when your friend has to order it after 100 degree weather and 3 drinks)
- The humidity of all those goddamned waterfalls and simulated rain frizzed my hair, a big extra F U to the rain forest café, I wasn't finished shopping yet, and yes, that does ruin my day until my Life Straightening Hair Day Comes Thank You Very Much.

Because we had not mocked the environment enough, we stopped by a World Market store. This is where people can buy 3rd world authentic crafts and, more importantly, chocolate from around the world -- in a gift store setting without having to brave the environment of a third world nation. It's like Zimbabwe without the flies or India without the beggars. Which is rather how the rainforest café is like the Amazon without the malaria. The world market has tribal music playing in air conditioned quiet. Do people care some kid went blind beading this bowl for 27 days straight for a chunk of goat meat and a nickel? No, it comes with a little note telling you about how much he appreciates your patronage. And there I am thinking what if Nabugu had a contagious disease...is it on my bowl? Could I write him back and be his pen pal?

Dear Leprosy Kid,
Thanks for the bowl. Please tell me that leprosy is not contagious or I am taking this back. Here is a nickel extra for your hard work.
Thanks,
Love Jenifer.
P.S. how do you not even blink when flies walk over your eyes?

I know this is very wrong and I still cry when I watch those feed this kid for 30 cents a day fundraisers, but I have homeless people in my own family. So after we left the rainforest café and got on the freeway, I said *"my cousin lives near here."* And Dom said *"your cousin lives in Orange County?"* No, my cousin does not live near the 405 freeway; he lives under it. He is homeless. No one in the family likes to admit this, because you see they are Jehovah Witnesses. They love knocking on total strangers doors and preaching the word of Jehovah, but they don't seem to mind their brother/son/cousin out there because he is not a JW. An extra special big F U to the JWs for that one. As we were driving back on the 405 with 3rd world chocolate and too much leftovers from the Rainforest Café I was wondering which freeway underpass he lived under and how do you exactly approach someone with no teeth who is your blood relation and say *"I am sorry you didn't take your medication...I am sorry none of us will let you live with us but you steal our things and our medication and you know, when you chase us around the house, it is not really appreciated. Here is a Plant Sandwich and a beaded bowl Nubugu made. Have a nice day."*
Somewhere the world has gone all wacky when you go to a fake rainforest café and come out with enough food to feed the homeless who have no addresses so you can't even find them. Homeless family members should have microchip tracking devices. Or at the very least a prepaid cell phones or something; we could call him...bring him

food. This is a touchy subject and he is my cousin, but without his medication he is basically like being around a Speed Freak Patrick Bateman. So don't crawl under the 405 freeway between Anaheim and Irvine because I can't guarantee your safety.

Then we stopped in Irvine...to go to that middle school. Eagle Run or Brookeside or Lakeside or Sweet Valley, it was some Judy Blume school where I know Deenie lives. Anyway, Domino has to talk to all these kids and she stuck all that makeup in a Black and Decker case. I am just staring at it and she screams "*WHAT? This is what Eric bought for the fashion show!*" So either she was the electrician or that huge thing was full of glitter. Gay men cannot shop for all things; let that be known now. Eric the drag queen bought the case. Possibly on purpose.

So here she is explaining to them how to apply makeup and possibly wire a house. She even gave a few kids makeovers, smiling like a spokesmodel whilst lying and telling them they all had one beautiful thing they could play up. like her name was Oprah, and I am thinking ...who is this person? But she is a Gemini and in case anyone has noticed, they have more personalities than Sybil.

There was this one little girl from band camp, and she wouldn't shut up. She kept saying "**BUT I PLAY THE FLUTE AT BAND CAMP I CAN'T WEAR LIP GLOSS!**" and I was waiting for her to say "one time at band camp" but she never did. Dom did their makeup all nice. They didn't look like when she did my makeup and made me look like Hustler. Then they all wanted to know what shape their eyes were, so Domino went around like some demented Miss MaryAnn and she told each and every one of them their eye shape. She even carried a mirror. She probably thought there was a camera and she was hosting

Romper Room. I would have said *"Well kids, you have two, work with that unless you have one of those Sandy Duncan eyeballs then I can't help you!"*

Then she told them about colors and how you could use them to accentuate and make your eye color *pop* out. Who wants their eyes to pop out is beyond me, it sounds painful. And entirely unnecessary to the band girl who had Marty Feldman eyes. So Domino told one her eyes would really pop out if she wore violet. Then she said that to the next one and by the 5th girl I was on to her. She was telling them all to use violet because she was tired. Somewhere in a middle school in Orange County, 25 Junior High girls showed up looking like someone socked them in the eye. It's all Domino's fault.

The school was 94% white and there was a little girl who had not paid for the class and she wanted a goodie bag and the teacher hissed SHE DIDN'T PAY FOR THE CLASS. I wanted to hiss back *"teachers who never wear makeup shouldn't give glamour classes!"* but since I made fun of the 3rd world bowl kid, I gave the little girl all the bags we had left. Okay, so it won't change the world but at least Lola has lip gloss now. You gotta start somewhere. Charity sweeties, charity.

And then a kid, with an entire bottle of glitter on her face came up and asked me if was there to put makeup on them too and asked for an autograph...this poor misguided child wanted an autograph from a total stranger in the corner who hadn't said a word. Please kid, I am not the mystery guest. I don't give seminars...so I just said to her *"Umm...WEAR VIOLET...just try wearing some violet shadow tomorrow!"* Yea, and I will be the woman writing about it. So she walked over to Dom and I see her leaning over shaking her head at the kid and then writing something down. The kid wanted her autograph. Hello, don't you people in Irvine give your kids role models? Your child just asked a total stranger on Xanax and carrying bottled water and wondering if her underwear is showing over the waistband of her trousers for an autograph and actually received one from a woman who is wearing two different colored socks.

Enter the Facemaster

I saw this contraption one time before on late night TV. You simply electrocute your face via 2 small jumpers plugged into a battery on the console. People pay money to get the same sensation I got as a child when my sister told me to lick a battery to see if it was still good. The theory is that it tones your face; it works out the muscles beneath the skin and tones them; you never work that part of your body out. Makes sense. I needed one. It was one of those _"Heyyyy, I need to dehydrate all our produce!"_ moments. Where for a moment, you envision all the dried banana chips and beef jerky you could produce from your very own kitchen, like Martha Stewart on speed. Except with this, you run electric shocks into your face. The Spa meets a mini version of The Green Mile.

But I got distracted by Whiny Nasal Woman on the Home Shopping Network, so I switched the channel before Suzanne could help me purchase something to shock my own face. When I was 20 something, I saw the Thighmaster and got one. It was blue and red and you closed and opened your legs on it. It was like a big spongy pretzel thingee that worked those hard to reach muscles. Yea, you mean the ones that anyone having the right sort of sex does without the aid of a spongy pretzel made in a Suzanne Somers factory. It went into a closet.

This is L.A. We work out. It's the law. If we refuse, they deport us somewhere dismal, like...that place Loretta Lynn came from... Butcher Holler.

Then came the next gadget, the Buttmaster. When I heard about the Buttmaster I just did not want it. Not something with a name that weird. Between you and me, I have no complaints about my butt. So far it has defied gravity. I like that in a butt. I do not need a Buttmaster, I am master of my own butt. Now that I am, thirty-five, I guess I should be thinking about more than my thighs or butt. Well actually, I did not think of this, but something led me to consider it.

On my last birthday, a Facemaster arrived. I thought what cheek someone has. On your first anniversary the traditional gift is paper, so it must be fair to assume that on your thirty fifth birthday, a Facemaster will arrive.

The argument was this. I really did not think I needed a Facemaster. I am 35, and I am not a sun worshipper, I do not drink alcohol often or do illegal drugs. I drink more water than a camel. I have maintained non-raisin like skin. But there is something very powerful about Suzanne Somers at 3am telling you how she puts conductive liquid on two jumpers and zaps her face back to youth. It had a very weird Frankenstein quality. There was something very horrorshow about the retinal flashes and twitches your body receives from the machine. And we all know if something hurts, it must be working. We already inject rat poison into people's wrinkles. They acid wash the face. They do burn peeling. We rip out hair by the root. What's a little shock to the face when Suzanne Somers is promising eternal youth? Maybe I would never buy makeup from a woman who still wears blue eyeliner, but I had trusted her with my thighs and my torso; so why not my face?

But getting A FACEMASTER in the mail on my thirty fifth birthday? What a cruel gift. Is someone trying to tell me something? So my first thought is to ask my friends if they ordered one for me. Most of them had not even heard of it, but I needed to find the culprit. It seemed I was the only dork up at 3am who had seen it. My second thought, after dismissing the first as too cruel, was 'did I order this in a sleeping pill induced haze at 3am? Am I honestly becoming this Joey Heatherton? Do I need to re-read Valley of the Dolls?'

When I finally realized that a roommate had ordered the thing and it was not some cruel thirty something birthday prank, I was okay. I was anticipating electrocuting my face. I wanted to zap any future wrinkles and scare them away. However, if you do not have any serious Keith Richards crevices to watch miraculously disappear, what do you get in the end except a face reddened by electric shock? The furrow I have -- only botox can save it now. So I was on to other uses. I have a very mean kitten that appears to be possessed. Could I exorcise the demon using a small electric current when she climbs me like a scratching post? Could I use this on unruly nephews and nieces?

'"*What do you mean you don't want to pick up your toys?*"
::ZAP:::
"*Yea, kid, I thought so. Suck it up and stop your crying. If Suzanne Somers can take it, so can you!*"

I have no idea where The Facemaster is now. I like to think it went to live with the Thighmaster and the Torso Trak and the food dehydrator and the jar of Nads. Everyone got bored watching their friends zap their faces. Although we did have fun sneaking up on people in deep slumber and shocking them awake. It could be a good thing to have around if your kids fall asleep in church. I think this is what Suzanne Somers had in mind. That is why it is small and battery operated. I am going to look for it and just carry it around with me. Salespeople, dentists, gynecologists, people who line their inner eyelid with blue eyeliner....there will be no mercy.

P.S. Please know that when you order anything from Suzanne Somers, an automated phone call with her voice calls you for eternity asking you to buy more stuff from her. That can freak a person out at 8am to answer the phone and hear Chrissie from Threes Company asking for you to buy more conductor fluid.

The Hermetic Crab
by Cameron Hill

It all started with a mean case of the crabs. Hermit crabs.

I was wandering through the razzle-dazzle of my home town's science fair. Semi-functional demonstrations mixed with hopeful charities, trying to collect the limited largesse of strained student and family budgets. Great fun for all the family. 'Cept the parents I guess. They spent their time keeping track of screaming children, and keeping little hands away from dangerous objects.

The cries of one misbehaving tyke drew my attention to a stand, whose primary commodity appeared to be crabs – one big and rather sadistic looking mud crab (responsible for the crying child) and a multitude of a smaller seashell clad variety. Hermit crabs, it turned out.

I eyed up the sign, written in a crab-like scrawl, identifying the price of the little crustaceans -- $30 a pop. I idly asked no one in particular, "Who in heck would want to pay $30 for a pet crab?"

The crab vendor chose this moment to come out of his shell and answer with an outraged expression painted across his heavy features.

"Why would you want a hermit crab? WHY? I'll tell you why! They're quiet, they'll eat anything and they live for thirty years! Clean and neat looking too! They don't shed fur, they don't rip up the furniture, and unlike bloody fish, they don't swim around with a trail of poop coming out of their butts!"

Charming mental vision.

He scooped up one of the larger crabs. It waved its claws indignantly, snapping them open and shut, making a quiet clicking noise.

"See this little bugger? 20 years old he is, and he hasn't crapped in all that time!"

I leaned in and squinted at the crab. It went for my nose with a razor claw. I jerked my head back.

"It *does* look constipated."

The vendor looked unimpressed. I shrugged and wandered a few paces away. Then I stopped. My girlfriend Kym's birthday was that week. I needed a present. I'd bet no one had given her a hermit crab before. Particularly a constipated one. I had a vision of her being distinctly unimpressed, but the amusement value...

I bought the crab. Kym was unimpressed. I had my amusement. We had an argument. I had to put up with three days of stony silence, then buy her expensive perfume.

So I inherited a pet crab. The blasted thing seemed rather smug.

Several weeks later I was out shopping at the local markets when a child ran past, closely pursued by a sweating shopkeeper. As I watched the chase, the child seemed to not be human at all.

"Come back here you brat!" screamed the shopkeeper as they both vanished round a corner.

I stood there blinking, and glanced about to see if anyone else had noticed. I decided I was mistaken and moved on. Problem was that throughout the rest of that day I could have sworn I saw a tree watching me and three pixies chasing small birds.

Upon arriving home the crab introduced itself in a broad Scottish brogue.

"Ah, I see by the spooked expression on yer mug that ye've woken up at last. I dinnae ken how ye slept so long as it is! I'm Angus. Yer a magician. I'm yer familiar and teacher."

Uh huh. Right. I needed a good night's rest. I shut its box and went to bed. When I peeled open my eyes I found the crab had got out of its box.

"Weel, laddie. This'll go a whole easier if ye just relax and listen. Yer a magician, and I'm here to teach ye what that means."

The crab waved its claws threateningly and fixed a stern and beady eye on me.

"Think o' magic like paintin' pictures. But, yer both IN the paintin' AND the painter. If ye wish to change somethin' in that paintin', ye need to draw it like. That's yer talent; ye can draw in new things. O' course ta do tha', ye need paint. Unfortunately fer you though, there's nae nice palette standin' by with lot's o' pretty colors waitin' to be dabbed and splattered aboot. Ye' have to use paint that's already in the picture."

Angus waved his claws enthusiastically.

"Fer example, say ye want fire? If ye had no fire in the picture, ye tain't goin' ta be able to do it. Tha' said, if ye got a lit match, ye can use it as 'paint' fer lightin' a candle while standin' 10 feet away or, if yer halfway capable, throwin' a ball o' fire at something."

The crab stopped his meandering and tilted his eyestalks up to look at me.

"Ye followin' this?"

I blinked. "Huh?"

The crab looked depressed.

"I can see this isn't goin' tae be easy is it?"

Angus started putting me through exercises – weeks passed and I lost weight. Angus seemed a little confused – thinking I've done some things I shouldn't have been able to do; but what's 'normal' where magic is concerned?

So my life came down to working during the day and practising magic at night, while trying to see enough of Kym to keep her from dumping me on grounds of neglect.

Except when I was at the psychiatrist.

It all became business as usual, until I found myself on the way to our local town markets, accompanying Kym on a shopping trip. A beat up car drove past, and I felt a chill run down my neck. Sitting in the driver's seat was a *thing*. It squeezed into the car in a way that would have been amusing had it not looked like a nightmare from the depths of hell. Grey skin, scars, and eyes that hadn't just stared into an abyss – they were the abyss.

Eyes that were tracking Kym.

We were all alone in the street. No passers by. Just us and the thing. It stopped the car and got out, and continued to get out. It was big! I turned ghostly white.

"Are you ok? What wrong?" she asked me. She shot a glance at the Beast, and smiled at it hesitantly. I didn't know what she was seeing but it obviously wasn't what I was seeing. I pulled Kym away, and started down the street. I couldn't think of anything except running.

The Beast leaped forward and backhanded me to the pavement. Kym screamed. I couldn't believe its strength, I felt like a cement truck had hit me. It shook Kym like a cat shakes a rat, and bundled her dazed form into the car. I tried to get to my feet. A dizzying black haze engulfed me.

I don't think I was out for long. I hurt all over and felt sick. I had no time to be sick. I rushed home, and ran to Angus' box. Wrenching off the lid I leaned down and started to babble.

"Angus, thisbighuge effing monster-thing grabbed Kym. I-I don't knowwheretheywent, youGOTTAhelpme..."

Angus nipped my nose. I yelped.

"Calm doon, laddie! Now, what did it look like?"

Angus somehow managed to furrow his shell in concentration as I described it.

"Right laddie. It's an ogre. Big, tough, dumber than a pile o' coo dung. Eats people, particularly bairns. Grab yer bag o' tricks and take me to where ye saw it."

So I did. I wandered up and down the street waving Angus about like a dousing wand. Passers-by stared. Why hadn't they been around when I needed passers-by?!? Three blocks away from the attack, Angus shouted, "A glamour!"

I looked about but had no idea what he was on about.

"Laddie, it's a common otherworld trick. Damn beast has grabbed a piece o' this place and hid it just outside reality. Strong stuff; hard to do for mortals, but it's instinctive tae the fae, and a few others. Concentrate. Try and see what ye think should be there – a street probably."

I concentrated. My eyes watered. I felt the start of a migraine. My attention started to wander. I shook my head and focussed... and a street was suddenly in front of me. I gasped and blinked. It was still there.

I stepped into a street that, given the style of the houses, must have been lost for forty years. The air smelled musty. Overhead the sky wavered and flickered, as if seen through a heat haze. The whole scene, its colors strangely washed out, reminded me of a faded photo. I was standing in the echo of a memory, stored in a forgotten album.

The street stretched ahead. The debris of shattered suburban quietude scattered across the road and the lawns, intertwined with the desiccated, mummified remnants of corpses.

I glanced at the nearest and flinched. The child had been horribly mauled. Tortured. Murdered at the very border. It must have been deliberate. The ogre must have let her drag her shattered body to the edge of escape.

"Aye laddie, tis a horror. Ye can end it though. Ye have that within ye. Brave it, and drag yon beastie doon. But do it sneaky like, as if ye were a godless Campbell."

I glanced at the bag hanging by my side. Angus peeked out. He waved his eyestalks and snapped his tiny claws decisively. I glanced back down the mausoleum street, squared my shoulders, and set off. I had an ogre to hunt.

I walked gingerly, stepping over broken bodies, their faces stretched forever in a rictus of pain and terror. Empty sockets stared into the flickering sky. Around me houses loomed, brightly painted despite the washed out atmosphere. In some, doors or windows had been smashed to kindling. Others were pristine, as if the owners had stepped out for just a moment.

I stumbled over the half-crushed wreckage of a child's tricycle; the clatter echoed up the entire street. I froze as the sound died away.

When I started to breathe, a gravelly voice boomed all around me.

"Fee. Fie. Foe. Fum. I'll taste the blood of an anguished man."

The air shook to a sinister laugh.

"Welcome Mage. I am glad you came."

"Great job, ye great clod-stompin' hairy coo!" squeaked Angus, "Ye've bloody blewn it noo! I said go sneaky like!"

"I thought you said these things were DUMB!" I shouted at the crab, "It thinks it's a frickin poet. That may be pretentious, but it's not DUMB!"

"Weel. Some of 'em are smart. I dinnae think it likely you'd run into a smart one. Bugger eh?" mumbled the misguided little cretin before hiding deep in my bag.

The gravelly voice laughed again. Houses shook around me. My teeth jarred in my skull and my ears started to bleed.

"I can smell your fear!" it gloated, "Come then wizardling. I'll grind your bones to powder and suck out your eyeballs. But I'll do it, oh... So... Slow. Your lovely and I are waiting in number 13."

I walked down the street towards that ill-fated number.

The grey warty monstrosity lumbered from the kitchen door. I wasn't sure how, but it managed to squeeze through without turning the doorframe to splinters. It loomed over me and grinned, revealing dirty gravestone teeth, slick with rotting blood. Its gums held rotting meat and maggots. The stench hit me like a tumbling brick wall.

It lifted one clawed slab of a hand, and gestured at me to come, as if it was an extra in a martial arts movie. I tried to imagine it relaxing in front of a Bruce Lee flick.

I threw my first spell. I blew a puff of air from my mouth, and ramped it up to hurricane speed. The huge beast staggered back, fell and rolled a dozen meters. How heavy was it? I'd expected more. I pursued it, passing the house containing Kym.

The Beast stood up, and leered mockingly.

I pulled out a lighter, flicked the action, and watched a feeble flame spring into life. I reached out to the fire, gathering its energy and essence. I fed it my rage and fear, and hurled the crackling wave of angry doom at the monstrosity.

The firestorm blasted down the street. Everything in front of me vanished behind a blazing wall of heat, the back draft blasted me from my feet, burning my skin, singeing my hair and sucking the air out of my lungs. I choked and blinked through tearing eyes. The street in front of me had been turned into a pyre, the very tarmac bubbling from the furnace blast.

The Beast stood in the midst of it, barely singed. It leered at me and laughed its booming bone-grinding laugh. I shook my head in denial, and then fled into a sturdy house, slamming and locking doors behind me. Panting, I sank to the floor.

Moments later the door and wall were hammered to splinters as the ogre came straight through, reaching for me with its dreadful hands. Panicking, I picked up a fallen brick multiplying the force and mass, and hurled it at its head. The brick smashed into it with an audible crack and actually knocked it over. I reached out and multiplied the force of the ogre's fall. It hit the ground with a titanic bang, and vanished through the floor.

I took a couple of breaths and looked into the cellar.

A pair of gleaming eyes stared up at me.

I whimpered and fled back to the street. I was exhausted. I was panicking. I had found more power than I had expected and it hadn't been nearly enough! I'd nearly blasted half a street to ash and cinders, and hit the thing with enough kinetic force to put it through a solidly built floor. It hadn't even had the good grace to say "Ouch!" With a crash, it emerged from the house. I could see that this time it was going to stop screwing about and finish it.

"That's it?" it roared, "I had hoped for a bit of entertainment, but if that's all you can offer, I'm just going to start peeling your scalp off!"

I fled to the edge of the inferno. I swung around and watched it advance. I glanced at the tortured bodies littering the street. This was really going to hurt. Kym would suffer as well.

Hurt...I could manipulate and multiply forces. Could I manipulate emotion? I acted. Grasped my own pain and exhaustion, attuned it to the deep suffering that was part of the damned place, and forced that blistered, screaming, soul deep horror into the core of the Beast.

The ogre staggered under this tsunami of torture. My own talent acting like petrol on a furnace.

It staggered and fell, eyes wide. Perhaps it had never before felt pain. That would explain its obsession.

Agony rose to a crescendo within me, filling me with a torture so intense it verged on pleasure. I fell to my knees and lost everything in a terrible haze. I could feel my skin flayed, my nails torn out, my eyes boiling, frangible bones smashing to shards, arms slowly wrenched from their sockets. I added magic to it and made the creature FEEL.

It was suffering the accumulated hurt of hundreds of painful deaths, multiplied by my magic. I almost stopped, then there was only pain, and the endless passing on of pain.

When awareness returned I found myself eyeball to eyestalk with Angus. He had been nipping my nose with his tiny claw.

"Aboot time laddie. I dinnae ken what ye did to yon monster. But it worked."

The street was even more a wreck; smashed walls and cratered tarmac attested to the Beast's desperation.

"'Twas like it went mad laddie. It staggered aboot roaring fit to bring doon the sky, dashing it's noggin against any hard surface it could find afore it clawed its own eyes out, and thrust its claws into the sockets."

Angus hesitated, as if not sure whether to continue, "Ye can be pretty damn vicious laddie."

I walked over to the huge corpse; partially covered under a fallen wall. Angus was right. Its head was cracked and bleeding from massive impacts. It had torn out its own eyes and much of its brain... I doubled over and retched.

After a time I stood and went looking for Kym.

She was bruised and battered but well, thank God. When she saw me she cried out in fear and hope. I kissed her, then started to tear feverishly at the rope binding her. How the damn ogre had managed such petite knots with its clumsy claws baffled me.

"It's ok, baby. It's dead," I said quietly, looking into her eyes. I could see she wanted to believe me.

"Aye lassie, yon beastie is slain. Yer safe now." Angus interjected. Kym looked in shock at the crab. Angus winked. An interesting trick for something with no eyelids.

Kym fainted.

"Oh aye! Tha' be right, she stays conscious all through being terrorized by a huge bairn eatin' ogre with a penchant fer bad poetry and then faints when she lays eyes on yoors truly!"

We staggered through my door. I carried Kym to the bedroom, and placed her gently on the mattress. I examined her for injuries – remarkably she seemed well, barring some bruises. I guess I'd got there in time, or perhaps the ogre wanted to torture us together. I considered falling into bed alongside her, but I had to talk to Angus.

"Angus, what the hell was that? How many of those things are there? Is this going to be a regular problem?"

Angus looked at me seriously from atop a stylish coffee table.

"Weel, laddie. I havnae been entirely honest wi' ye. I dinnae think that ogre attacked ye randomly, though they do like tormentin' wizards and magical folk."

I snatched Angus up and held him at eye height.

"Alright you little bugger, talk. Kym nearly died 'cause of that thing! If you know something I need to hear it."

Angus wilted.

"Ok laddie...Weel, about 600 years ago, I was apprenticed to a great magician named Walter o' the Dale. He was like ye, laddie, far stronger than he should hae been, and able tae do some strange things, even by wizard's standards. He didnae learn as fast as ye tho, or improvise like ye. Ye're very strange that way, laddie."

"600 years!?! How?"

It started to rain outside.

"Hush, laddie! I'm getting' tae it." snapped Angus, "Now one fell day, along came this other magician, a laird o' the Douglas clan. He's well known and feared in wizarding circles – we call him Douglas the Black, or just, The Douglas. Don't get me wrong, the Douglas' are a fine clan, by and large, but this Douglas was steeped in dankest evil. He was one o' the order of Harvesters. These Harvesters kill magicians, and otherworld beasties, and bind their souls and power into some sort o' talisman. Douglas the Black used an amulet, and he murdered a lot o' powerful wizards, and many fae. He killed my master and took his soul."

Angus' voice started to crescendo, and let me tell you, a crescendo-ing hermit crab is almost an intimidating sight.

"As I stood in my masters blood that day I swore that I'd nae rest until I had my vengeance! That I'd see Douglas' black soul sent to hell to suffer forever!"

Thunder boomed. Naturally.

"Well, I tain't rested laddie. I'm still here! Guess that oath had real power."

I wet my lips, "Er, is that how you became a crab? Did this Douglas guy transform you?"

Angus looked slightly exasperated.

"Well, actually, it's kind 'f embarassin', laddie'. I'd rather nae…"

'Tell me, Angus,' I growled.

"I did that meself. Ye see Walter had this other apprentice – Willy. We had a little rivalry goin', and one day I decided to turn him into a toad. I stole a spell from my master's book and cast it on him while he was sleepin'. 'Cept I got it wrong. The spell got me, and fer some reason I ended up a crab! What kind o' Scot ends up a hermit crab! Anyway, mebbe my master could hae helped me… After he'd finished laughin' in any case…But that very mornin' was when the Douglas killed him. Killed Willy, too. Probably would hae killed me, but I was just a crab. Doin' crab things. Not worth botherin' with."

I just stared. I opened my mouth. I closed it. I shook my head.

"Well how does all this tie in with the bloody ogre?"

"Douglas can't cram an unlimited number o' souls into that accursed amulet. He only wants the best. That means he needs tae see how good his targets are. Facin' a beastie like yon ogre is a nice test. If it'd eaten ye' then ye'd have been an unworthy victim fer 'is dastardliness. In addition, ye should be nicely softened up, weakened fer days after such a battle. I'd guess he contacted it and ensured it came after ye'. Probably promised it somethin' nice, besides torturing ye that is. Since yer still alive he'll be by sometime soon."

'Great. Here I was thinking I could maybe rest, and then get yelled at by Kym…Actually, facing a depraved black magician may be preferable."

I leaned in close to Angus.

"One more question, how did you end up with me?'

"Laddie, of all the wee niggling troubles faced by a hermit crab fightin' a 600 year long vendetta 'gainst a demonic magician whose disgustin' soul belongs in the blackest pits o' hell, organizing tae end up the only magic crab in a box at yer local science fair was not among the more difficult ones."

Fine! He didn't need to get smart.

"So how do we off this guy?" I asked.

A cough sounded from behind us. Angus and I looked at each other like children caught being naughty. We slowly turned around. Kym stood watching us.

"I heard it all," She said, "I want in."

Somehow, despite shock I managed to squeak, "All?"

She leveled a loaded finger at me.

"Be quiet you. First we deal with this evil wizard. Then you and I are having a little...Talk." I gulped, "Then I'm going to cry. Then have a drink. Probably after that I'll see a doctor."

My, she seemed to have adapted remarkably well to nearly being eaten by a murderous beast.

It wasn't long before we could act - I recovered much of my strength in a day. Angus was astonished, but pleased. It meant that we had a small chance of fighting this battle.

My primary concern was finding him – seemed to me that someone like that wouldn't be easy to detect by magic. I was wrong. Angus said that he'd be staying at a hotel called 'The Hermitage'. Every city had one. Kind of like every city had a restaurant called 'La Bella Vista.' He asserted that the Douglas, being a wizard, wouldn't be able to resist the synchronicity of staying at a place so named. Apparently, in his early days, he'd been the laird of a castle by that name in Scotland.

This also meant that Angus had already cooked up a plan, which needed only a little tinkering with Kym along. Damn thing sounded dodgy as hell to me, but I couldn't think of a better one, and neither could Kym. So we checked the phone book – and found it. Guess the crab was right.

Thus, by the next evening, Kym, Angus, and I had arrived at the foyer of a very nice hotel. Shining marble, gold trim (but only enough to be tasteful), and subtle sculptures abounded. Angus sniffed, said it looked nothing like the brooding lump of stone it was named for.

Under Angus' instruction I did a little Jedi mind trick on the manager, and we ascertained that a Douglas was indeed occupying the penthouse. Using my little magic, we were able to score one(1) maid's outfit, and one(1) silver tray, complete with dome.

I told you it was a dodgy plan.

Minute's later Kym was looking perky in the maid's outfit. I didn't want her to do this, but she had insisted. Stamped her foot in fact. On to mine. Ow.

We took the elevator up to the hall outside the penthouse. Clutching the tray, Kym kissed me lingeringly, took a deep breath, and then sashayed down the hall. I hated to see her leave, but I didn't mind watching her go (Oh alright. I agree, it was no time for lechery but she's cute.) I slipped out of sight behind a handy pillar, and held my breath.

I heard her knock.

"Room service! I have your dinner!" she sang huskily. I frowned, she was overdoing it. Of course he hadn't ordered dinner, but she could improvise. We hoped.

The door opened, and I heard a low conversation, and a flirtatious giggle. Oh for crying out loud, it was like a bad TV show.

I heard the door close. Silence ruled. I risked a glance around the pillar, and found the corridor empty. She was in.

Anxiously I popped some bubble gum and started chewing furiously. I advanced implacably up the corridor, trying to feel like some sort of conquering hero.

With bubble gum.

I stopped outside the door. I could hear discussion and a giggle. A moment later I heard Kym cry out.

Time to move!

I punched the air, magnifying the force of the gesture, and focussing it onto the door. I could have used the key, but it wouldn't have been nearly as dramatic. The portal shattered with a crack and fell inwards, revealing a beautifully furnished room. Standing in the center of the room was a large wooden table, elegantly carved out of some sort of fine ebony. A tall, well-muscled man of indeterminate age stood holding Kym's hand in what was obviously an uncomfortable (for her) grip. His head snapped around, his eyes falling upon me.

His gaze was like a concussive bomb. Ageless horror pumped directly into my soul. Not pain, but *wrongness*, filth, rot, and dead things bloating. That and *hatred*. I nearly vomited. I nearly lost my gum.

Through my nausea I noticed the layers of magical wards. Kinetic forces, electricity, heat, others I couldn't identify… He was nearly invulnerable to magical or physical attack. But only nearly.

Kym screamed and jerked away. I tried to pull myself together and cast my spell, but Douglas' hands snaked out. He was *fast*. He made a lifting and gripping motion with one hand, and a chopping motion with another. I felt magic weaving together.

An incredible force had clenched around my throat and hauled me into the air as something chopped down between my magic and I. Suddenly a strange sense of empowerment that I'd been feeling for weeks, and hadn't even noticed, was gone.

Douglas watched me with inscrutable hollow eyes; his sallow features blank. I felt like I was being regarded by some sort of hell-born alien insect. A moment passed. I hung in the air quietly choking. His head tilted to the side and he opened his mouth to say something…

Then he jerked his head back and hissed in pain as Kym sprayed pepper spray into his eyes. He doubled over, and his magic fell away. I struck.

I blew a large, ripe, cherry flavored bubble. You heard me right. I channeled that growth concept at a target under the silver dish.

Douglas stood suddenly, already shrugging off the spray's effects and backhanded Kym. She stumbled away, thankfully he hadn't used any magic on her. We could only have moments before he did. He pointed one finger at her, and another at me. Something very unpleasant was about to happen.

I completed my spell. A loud clattering sound rang out at as the silver dome impacted on the roof, and then a very large claw settled around the evil sorcerers chest.

"I hope yer mother can sew," said a rhino sized Angus, as he lifted his old foe into the air, "'Cause this'll need stitches."

And he brought Douglas's head crashing down onto his shell. Closest thing a hermit crab can manage to a Glasgow kiss I guess.

There was a loud crack, and Douglas' head rebounded. He was momentarily dazed, but that was about it. His wards were too strong for him to hurt much.

"Get the freakin' *amulet*!!!" I screamed.

Angus's other claw ripped away Douglas' shirt. Shining on his chest, like a malevolent dark pearl, was the evil talisman.

The magician started to cast something. Desperately I hit him with what I hoped was a functional version of the magic severing spell. It (metaphorically speaking) rang off his sorcerous shield, but the impact slowed his casting…

Angus' claw tore away the amulet. He flung it to me, then got blasted aside and shrunk back to normal as Douglas hammered him with lethal sorcery. The evil wizard swung to me with a snarl on his face, hand reaching out…

I caught the amulet, revolted at its icy touch, but filled with immense power. I could hear the clamoring spirit voices within screaming for vengeance; their rage filling me.

Something tugged viciously at my heart. I felt it's beat stutter. Darkness flickered at the edges of my vision. Desperately grabbing the first random concept, I cast a spell.

Douglas the Black reared back. My amulet fuelled spell cut through his defenses like a cat through hot butter. He staggered a couple of steps, his alien, echoing eyes widening as his flesh started to run.

"I'm meltiiiiinnnnggg!" he gurgled as he dissolved into a faint amber colored liquid. A smoky scent filled the air. He subsided into a puddle on the impeccable marble floor.

Angus, remarkably unhurt given he'd been engulfed in an inferno a moment ago, wandered over to the puddle. Kym and I just stared at it. We both looked at Angus.

'I think you distilled him.' stated the crab.

A few days later, Kym and I were standing atop a lovely wooded hill, in the fading light of a summer's day. I hugged her to me, then ceremoniously up-ended the bottle of Black Douglas onto the grassy soil.

Ahem.

Under the pressure of screaming spirits, confronted by a guy named Douglas the Black…Well, I'd just had to improvise. It made sense!

Sort of.

Anyway, Angus stated we couldn't be sure someone that powerful would stay dead unless we delivered him to a place of true power owned and watched by his most hated enemies.

So we sponged him up, stuck him in a bottle, and here we were – standing on a fairy mound. Kym could now see creatures from the otherworld. Angus say's that's fairly normal – her eyes have been forcefully opened, so to speak.

Oh. There was one outstanding bit of business. Destroying that amulet. It was an artifact of power and that would not be easy. It could wait a few days.

As the last drop ran out of the bottle, I gazed up at the brilliantly colored sky, and enjoyed the warm breeze on my face. Seems I'd have a chance to understand my magic better. Both Angus and Kym were fine. She hadn't even had that Talk with me. Maybe she'd forgotten. I can always hope.

"The pixies are playing!" she said, "The pixies are playing!"

I turned and looked where she was pointing. They certainly were. We stood and watched them for a time, as the warm evening closed in.

Head Drippers
by Robert Steussi

I, Phillip Selfridge, M.A., Master of Arts-Journalism, Northwestern University, 1986, do hereby affirm that all events described herein are true. In January, 2002, I committed myself to Emerson-Palmer Psychiatric Hospital near Palm Springs, California, not because I was emotionally disturbed, but rather to test a proposition that had long troubled me. Could a sane person, committed to a mental hospital, prove himself sane afterwards and be released? Little did I know that my research would uncover.

Posing as Phil Selfridge, a community college professor suffering from vague symptoms of emotional distress, including excessive sweating and dry mouth, I made the necessary arrangements and drove myself up into the Lost River Mountains to Emerson. The upscale private hospital, operated under the aegis of Savitas United, nestled in a lush, irrigated stretch of grass along the meandering Sausalito River, its gleaming blue glass and aluminum architecture redolent of a plush resort or a health spa for wealthy matrons. The only discordant note came from a warning regarding the hidden, electrified fence that circled the perimeter, and a military-looking security guard.

After a brief wait I was ushered into Dr. Melrose Parker's suite by Nurse Anna Bohachick, a massive, well-scrubbed woman with a cheerful face and muscular legs. Dr. Parker rose at once from behind his huge, walnut desk and shook my hand, as he gestured towards an expensive black-leather armchair.

"And now what can we do for you, Phillip?" Dr. Parker said in a reassuringly deep baritone. He radiated an aura of solidity from his bald crown to his hairy-knuckled fingers.

"I have been troubled by voices," I said. "The tension has interfered with my work, and I think a period of brief respite would be in my best interest. My friends suggested Emerson."

"Certainly. Stress reaction, eh? I understand; intervals of depression can be devastating." Dr. Parker smiled benignly and gave me an encouraging look as we discussed my background and symptoms. After an hour, Dr. Parker steepled his fingers and said: "Phillip, I don't think there's anything here that we can't treat with medication, but I agree that a brief hiatus from your work duties might be in order. You'll find Emerson a total stress free environment—no telephones, no fax machines, no computers--just basic human communication. While you're settling in, we can run a battery of tests to ascertain what we're dealing with. Now if you're in agreement, there's paper work and insurance forms for you to fill out. I'll just turn you back over to Nurse B., and she'll lead you through the paper work. I sincerely hope you'll enjoy your stay."

After a firm handshake, Nurse Bohachik ushered me out of the office and issued me a pair of soft blue pajamas; I officially became a patient at Emerson Psychiatric assigned to a private bedroom on Ward 2B South.

I soon met my neighbors on the ward. Mrs. Selvy had tried to decapitate her husband with a string trimmer. Although she was the most pleasant lady, a constant stream of unintelligible dialogue sputtered from her mouth. Arthur Cromby, a tiny man with wire-rimmed accountant's glasses, was perpetually playing spirited games of checkers against himself. He punctuated the game with cursing and angry outbursts. Madame Warshosky was the most imposing. Hatchet-faced, she widened out from the neck into a grotesque pear with gigantic hips and even larger thighs. She spent most of the day sitting in the corner crying or trying to cadge cigarettes.

And then there was swaggering Hubert Warley, a hulking motorcycle-gang type, with tattoos on his face and neck and giant safety pins in his eyebrows. He was perpetually on the brink of explosion as he strutted about the ward in jockey shorts.

After I met my inmate friends, Arthur Cromby became my favorite. From him I learned that the staff was trying to poison his food and that Hubert Warley was an undercover agent for the ATF; other than those two delusions, Arthur's mind functioned soundly.

"What do you think of this stem cell business," he asked one afternoon.

"I hadn't thought much about it," I said looking up from my copy of *Time*. Mainly I'd been preoccupied with my bid for release. My final test was scheduled for later that afternoon, and if I lied enough in my responses, Dr. Parker was certain to diagnose me not as a stress reaction, but as schizophrenic.

"I said - what do you think of this stem cell business??" Arthur repeated. "You know Parker and these other sons of bitches are very much involved in stem cell research, transgenic procedures. I don't trust them as far as I can throw an elephant. They're up to something. Something that would boggle the mind."

"What?" I raised an eyebrow.

"Cloning? Or God knows what. The staff has an agenda. You take that Schultz guy."

"I haven't met him."

"Oh you will. You will. He's one of their offspring. In fact, here he comes."

Before I could get an explanation, a burly attendant, presumably Schultz, grabbed me by the shoulders and told me "they" wanted me upstairs for testing. Insisting I ride in a wheelchair, he bounced me in one as if I was a rag doll.

On the way to the testing center, we passed by a locked ward.

"What's it like in there?" I asked. He laughed out loud.

"You really want to know what it's like with those crazy-ass head-drippers?"

"Crazy-ass head-drippers?"

"You heard me, Selfridge. Here let's take a peek," he said. To my surprise he pulled out a ring of keys, unlocked the huge metal door and wheeled me inside. At the same moment a fire alarm sounded.

"Jesus! I got to go!" Schultz shouted and dashed off, leaving me sitting opposite a teenager who was banging his head on the wall. Overcome with curiosity about "head-drippers," I decided to look around. I rolled myself past the headbanger to a room from where I heard moaning. The door was propped open and I could see an emaciated patient with a wild Afro lying on a table under an intense beam of light. Dr. Parker and two assistants, chattering in a language I couldn't identify, surrounded him. A huge machine that I would liken to a dentist's drill hung over the patient. Suddenly Dr. Parker seized the drill (if I can call it that) and probed the patient's forehead. Whether there was any anesthetic involved I cannot say, but the patient did not cry out.

The drill sutured back the skin of the patient's forehead and Dr. Parker's blue-gloved hands lifted out something the size of a rabbit. The emergent rabbit-thing gave a strange cry and instantly the attendants hustled it into an incubator that was humming like a sewing machine.

Shocked and uncertain by what I had just witnessed, I rolled myself away from the doorway. A moment later

Schultz came dashing back with an alarmed look on his face.

"What the hell are you doing in this area, Selfridge? I didn't leave you off here. I ought to break your neck. This part of the ward is off limits to patients," he cried. "Didn't you see that sign?"

I looked to where he had pointed, and it was true. I hadn't seen the sign at all. His pupils narrowed to pinpoints. Schultz grabbed me by the neck again and gave me a fierce shake.

"You ever pull a stunt like that again, and you'll regret it."

"I'm sorry," I said, feeling a deep thrust of fear. Schultz became as close-mouthed as a coffin as he rolled me on towards the testing center. My curiosity piqued, I was determined to stay at Emerson longer and learn its secrets.

As the bearded psychologist showed me the series of inkblots, I was very careful to see only violence, absurdity, and twisted Oedipal themes certain to mark me as schizophrenic. Apparently my ruse succeeded as Dr. Parker called me to his office the next morning.

"Phillip, the tests suggest that you are suffering from much more than just stress. You have a borderline schizophrenic condition. I'd say you'll need to stay with us for at least sixty days, and then if your medication is effective, you should be able to return to your normal life by autumn. Do you have any questions?"

I shook my head no and for the first time I noticed his left hand had a tiny sixth finger, loosely attached at the base of the pinky. I wondered how I had not noticed before. The opportunity was never better to bring up what I had seen on the violent ward the preceding day. Shock crossed Dr. Parker's face followed by a benign smile.

"Phillip," he said, "what you accidentally witnessed was electric shock therapy. It's quite effective. Perhaps in your agitation, you imagined certain elements. Visual hallucinations are not uncommon with your diagnosis."

When Schultz escorted me back to the ward, I found Arthur Cromby playing checkers in a foul mood.

"The son of a bitch has been cheating again," Arthur cried concerning his imaginary opponent as I sank into a leather chair.

"Arthur, listen. I saw something weird today. You're not going to believe this, but Schultz left me on a locked ward upstairs, and I saw Parker doing surgery on a patient's head, and I swear to God a fetus came out."

Arthur didn't even bother to look at me.

"You're finally catching on, Selfridge. This place is phony. Parker and his gang are doing experiments on the patients upstairs. What you saw was nothing."

"What do you mean nothing?"

"I mean the shit that happens at night is incredible. They're taking fetuses out of heads by the hundred."

"What are you talking about, Arthur? Who's they?"

"Parker and the hospital staff. You don't think they're actually human beings do you? They're wearing clever disguises. The fuckers are from another planet. Trivestia they call it."

"That's crazy, Arthur," I said.

"You think so, Selfridge? You're pretty smart, aren't you? Tonight I'll show you who's crazy. I'll take you down in the basement and let you see for yourself."

"If what you say is true, it could be dangerous."

"God, you're a slow learner for a guy who's not even nuts." Cromby shook his head. "Now listen…" Then he explained our predicament.

Shortly after midnight, he gave my shoulder a shake. "Time to go exploring," he said. "Just remember if anyone asks us what we're doing, go totally bonkers. Put on your best wigged-out act. These extra-terrestrials are smart, but they ain't subtle."

I followed Arthur down the dimly lit corridor of hospital beds and through the heavy, locked metal door. In a few tense minutes we were down the hall and taking the freight elevator to the basement. Embalming fluid assaulted my nostrils as Arthur and I stumbled through the darkness.

"Arthur," I whispered, "We'd better go back. There's no lights. I don't like the looks of this."

"Jesus Christ, Selfridge, are you a man or a mouse?" Arthur barked. "I told you I know my way around this dump."

"I don't understand, Arthur. If you know how to get out of here and you hate it so much, why don't you escape?"

"Why would I escape? There's nothing on the outside but ATF agents. I'm better off here."

I tried to stay within touching distance of Cromby as we stumbled across an earthen floor. Then suddenly Arthur kneeled, put his ear to a door, fiddled with the lock, and pushed it open.

We were gazing into a roomful of corpses illuminated by recessed purple lighting emanating from the floor. The naked cadavers were lying on operating tables. Hordes of strange fetal creatures, no bigger than rabbits, clustered about their heads like suckling pigs.

"My God!" I gasped. "What's going on?"

"This is their ballgame. Those poor stiffs lying there dead are former mental patients. Parker and his associates use the brains of the dead as incubators for their offspring. Then after the patients die, they leave them down here to serve as feeding titties for the newborn."

"You can't be serious about this, Arthur?"

"If I'm not serious... what the hell do you think you're staring at?"

Before I could answer, yellow light suddenly flooded the basement room. The corpses and the feeder fetuses were no longer visible. My heart leaped into my throat; I turned around and stared into the faces of Dr. Parker, Nurse Bohachick, and Schultz. Their daylight faces had transformed into gray, cheek-less masks with huge domed foreheads.

"What a pleasure to see you here again, Cromby, and I see you've brought a guest."

Dr. Parker seemed totally at ease.

"Don't give me that pleasure shit, son of a bitch." Nurse Bohachick raised what looked like a cigarette lighter and flicked its triggering mechanism. Arthur was instantly fastened to the walls, quivering with electricity. I don't like to think about his screams because I saw the blue fire shooting behind his teeth and erupting from his groin.

"Now for you, Selfridge," Parker said. "I thought I made it clear to you during your orientation that certain areas of the hospital are off-limits. As a result of your defiance, we will subject your testicles to electric shock."

I inhaled sharply, trying to think of some excuse. Nothing would come.

"In addition to the shock, it's my duty to inform you that the results of your latest tests are in. You are verging on a very severe psychosis with signs of paranoid schizophrenia. It will now be necessary to confine you on a locked ward."

You don't fight back against electrical weapons, so I took the testicular shock. Schultz laughed while I was still writhing with pain; he dragged me down to the locked ward and pushed me inside.

I spent the night huddled by the door, clutching a blanket. In the morning I met my dorm mates – cutters, tangent talkers, and feces eaters – who all had one element in common. The left side of their heads was either bandaged or healing after invasive surgery.

That first morning, I met a strange man kneeling down drinking out of a toilet.

"Hey," he cried glancing up, "you're new, ain't you?"

I nodded in amazement at this seven-foot tall man.

"You want to see my incision?" he shouted. "I'm Sterly Brown!"

"I don't know, Mr. Brown."

"Hell, it's a beauty," Sterly cried, ripping the bandages off his head and hurling them to the tile floor. His thick fingers ripped back the flaps of the wound so that I could see into the gangrenous cavity. Deep within lay some healthy dark, pulsing tissue that was obviously his brain.

"You're going to get one of these operations before long. Everybody here does. It don't hurt none."

"But why? I don't understand. Why do they do it?"

"For them there little embros of theirs. They opens up your head, puts one of them little buggers inside, and he can feed right off your brain tissue. When he gets up to a pound, they take him on out and sew you up."

"What happens to the embryos?"

"They ain't embros anymore. They's little babies. Hell I don't know what they do with them then. Takes 'em back to their home planet I reckon. You know the nice thing?"

I shrugged my shoulders.

"They always name the baby after you."

"How nice," I said, trying to understand what madness would drive our captors to use the brains of madmen as incubators. Conditions on their planet must be strange and inhospitable, but nothing could be more perverted.

"That's easy," Sterly laughed when I asked, "nobody gives a shit if we ever come back. If we die feeding a kid, the hospital just says we died of natural causes."

With a huge grin, Sterly dipped his head back in the toilet bowl. "Want me to get you a drink while I'm down here? We're allowed to take all the water we want. I generally take a gallon or two every day."

"No, that's nice of you, but I don't want a drink," I said. I noticed Schulz hovering behind me, carrying a concrete-filled rubber hose.

"They want you upstairs, Selfridge, asshole," Schultz said, grabbing me by the collar. "You'll have to leave the water man alone to finish his business."

An instant later Schultz forced me onto a freight elevator and whisked me up to an operating room on the fourth floor. Dr. Parker, Nurse Bohachick, and a half dozen other technicians were waiting for me. Dr. Parker's rubber-gloved fingers felt around my skull. Shultz held me roughly to the operating table; Nurse Bohachick forced a mask over my nose and mouth. The last thing I remember hearing was Dr. Parker explaining that Cromby had been executed. I would be rendering a great service to his planet where women found themselves unable to nurse infants in the conventional fashion.

When I awoke, Nurse Bohachick showed me a photograph of the embryo implanted in my brain.

"We'll call him, Phillip," she said, "he's a boy. Schultz is his father, so you can feel very proud."

I said nothing, thinking of the horror that lay ahead. The tiny fetus would be feeding on my brain. I would be no better than a captive wasp feeding a tarantula's offspring.

And so it has been, for the six months of incubation. Luckily for me, the procedure is pain-free although there is an uncomfortable itching when the child moves.

Whether or not I shall die here for knowing too much, I have no idea. Shultz has begun to refer to me as the Godfather of his child; I must say I've begun to develop an affinity for the man. Knowing he has two stomachs and two hearts sometimes bothers me; yet he protects me from Hubert Warley. Also, Madame Warhosky is an excellent partner for bridge so long as I'm able to provide her with an occasional cigarette, and don't invite Hubert Warley to play. My head wound has begun to heal nicely. Nurse Bohachick says that I may soon be ready to become a feeder.

Why I spent so much time trying to poke my own eyes out, I cannot say. Dr. Parker suggests it is a guilt syndrome associated with my curiosity having been instrumental in causing the death of Arthur Cromby. All I know is that I am very astute at calculating the time until the next meal, and very excited about the photographs that Schultz has promised to show me of my godson, who is learning to walk in electric power shoes. I only wish Trivestia were not so far, far away. I could stroke my namesake's head and watch the lad grow to maturity.

Something Funny is Going On
by Brian Rosenberger

War Journal Entry 14/12

Fuck. Screwed up today. Typical patrol. Eyes and ears open. All senses on the high end of the dial. Body on full alert. Juicing on caffeine and legal stimulants. Weapons cataloged, cleaned, and cocked. Not expecting anything but always prepared. Always. I heard laughter. Not the sound of kids playing or schoolgirls with the giggles. This was much heavier, throaty, almost raw. Artificial laughter is one of the tell tale signs. We remember. How can we forget the laughter as they killed our friends, our family, our town. You don't forget the hair, the costumes, the frozen smile, death in their lifeless eyes. I was at the Big Top Burger. You don't forget. You never forget.

Approached on its blindside. One look at that holly jolly costume, the big boots, the kids drawn in like moths to the flame by that big belly laugh, and I knew my only option. I drew. Five shots at close range. I take no chances. Small entrance, big exit. Always aim for the nose. Feel bad about the kids seeing blood splattered. Would feel worse if it were their blood. God bless deer slugs and a little American ingenuity. It dropped in mid laugh; its rosy cheeks sucking wind, its belly quivering like Jell-O. The fake beard came off as it fell, struggling for help. But we know they are masters of disguise, mimics without peer. They've got chameleon DNA, reptile instincts. They know how to blend. You've got to be colder, smarter, and better than they are. DTA. Don't trust anyone. Words to live by.

I remember the bicycle I got on Christmas the year before they came. Mom always loved Christmas. The crusade continues.

War Journal Entry 23/12

I hate shoppers. I hate Christmas shoppers. I really hate Christmas shoppers with fucking cell phones. Don't these poor bastards realize their lives are at stake? The shit we could tell them would bug out their color contact wearing eyes. They drive around in their gas-guzzling mastodons on wheels with their damn phones attached to their ears just to get a better deal on little Steve's toys. They cut me off three times today. It makes me sick. Well, I've got news for you buddy; your name's on top of the menu and it's an all you can eat buffet. Hurry, Hurry, step right up. See the non-seeing, non-believing, blind-in-both-eyes, typical American male. Can you say endangered? Fucking cell phoned, mind controlled bastards.

Cell phone equals mind control?

Possibility.

War Journal Entry 2/1

I wanted to write more yesterday but was still too hung over. And a happy New Year to you too.

This time of year is meant to be with family. They took my family away. I was left with only my name, my inheritance, and my desire for vengeance. It's been a nightmare merry-go-round ever since.

Sometimes I still can't believe. I can understand why so many of the surviving town folk of Crescent Cove refuse to talk about what happened. It's easier to forget. It's easier to pretend they aren't out there. Just look the other way. The government didn't even have to cover up. Self-preservation and the denial factor went into hyper drive. People wanted to talk but they didn't know what to say. The ones that did were locked up and labeled disturbed. Well, Jesus H. Christ, when you see your family cotton candied to death in front of you, I'd say you have the right to be disturbed.

I enlisted to get some answers and learn the art of war. One visit to the hardware store and I've got an arsenal. I can take a guy out five different ways, without him realizing it, without even breaking a sweat. My questions were red taped from every angle by the top brass on down. It was like Valentines Day. So many sugar coated responses, so many flat out lies. When I asked the big question, where did all the people go, it was always the same stock answer -- people disappear everyday. Well, no shit. Why do you think they're disappearing? It's them. They're responsible for more faces on milk cartons than you can imagine.

I feel sorry for the masses. They have no idea. They do the nine to five thing or eight to six thing, or whatever it takes to pay the bills. They have no purpose. They just feed the machine. One way or another. Not me. I know my purpose. I have a mission. I'm a man on a mission. I won't stop. No brakes allowed.

War Journal Entry 5/3

I've been traveling, hitting all the little sideshows and amusement parks. There's more than you think. I almost plugged a pair of mimes last week. Their act was so pathetic they had to be human. You can't fake that kind of crap. You never realize how big this country is until you see from the road. You don't realize how many damn bugs there are either. I could have scrapped them off the windshield using a putty knife. Thick as Mom's mashed potatoes.

I got a tip from one of my contacts. He's a UFO nut who makes a mean pot of chili. He's a news hound. Magazines and newspapers and tapes all over. We don't see eye to eye on many things. His theory about Atlantis being covered by the Gobi Desert is a crock. We both agree there's stuff going on that is kept very low on the general public's radar screen. Through the electronic grapevine, he heard about some farmer who found a crop circle in his field. No big deal right. Only the crop circle was in the shape of a smiley face. You don't see the talking faces on the national news networks broadcasting that little factoid, do you? Stick that in your Big Top Burger and see how it tastes.

War Journal Entry 6/3

I still have nightmares. Sometimes I dream I'm at the dentist. I'm strapped in, hooked up to the laughing gas. As I'm about to go under, I see this chalk skinned, pasty-faced monstrosity reach into my mouth with its four-fingered hand and yank out a rubber chicken. The chicken has my mother's face.

I no longer go to movie theatres. The smell of popcorn sickens me.

War Journal Entry 8/3

The crop circle was a bust. Damn tourists had trampled the area. Nothing to see. The farmer was still charging admission. Five bucks a pop to see stomped on corn stalks. I guess it beats working. He took my money with a gap-toothed smile. A waste of time this trip, except I did pick up a new laser scope at a gun show. Bang. Bang.

War Journal Entry 8/5

A bit of a scare today. I thought I was being followed by one of those damn Mini Cooper cars. Damn things look like toys. Turned out to be some young blond more interested in applying her mascara than chasing my ass. Too bad as she was very pretty. She can tailgate me anytime. Still, you can never be too careful. We know they prefer compact cars.

War Journal Entry 3/5

I haven't had much time to write. I needed to regroup, rethink my mission. Some fucker stole my notebook. Year's worth of notes in some idiot's hands. He probably just threw it away. A blueprint for survival gone just like that.

But there is a ray of sunshine. I was having breakfast when the notebook was stolen. I went to the bathroom and then... poof. Gone. But my eggs were still there. So was the local newspaper. The headline said a new fast food joint was opening tomorrow. It's going to be the biggest in the area, complete with an indoor/outdoor playground. There's going to be prizes and a costume contest. There's even going to be a parade. They love parades. It's like candy. The occasion doesn't matter. I've seen them at St Patrick's and Opening Days. They can't resist.

Since Crescent Cove, they are more subtle. They don't display themselves openly. They've gotten better at passing as human. That's why I didn't realize it before. All this time it was staring at me in the face.

I'll be at the opening.

War Journal Entry 4/5

Today is the day. I'm ready. Everything is cataloged, cleaned, and cocked.

To beat your enemy, you have to become your enemy. Crescent Cove haunts me. I will never have a normal life until they are extinct. I know this as I apply the pancake make up. I fluff out the multi colored curls of my wig. I pull on the mismatched golf trousers I picked up at a thrift store. The oversized shoes I'll put on when I'm there. It's humanly impossible to drive wearing them.

I imagine what it will be like, the laser scope targeting the face, one trigger away from making the red nose even redder, white stained crimson.

I hope there is a gaggle of them.
I have a mission. I have a destination.
The Golden Arches. Today and every day after.

Clob
by Michael Stone

This is a story about how I found faith - faith as opposed to belief - and like many stories, it begins with boy meets girl.

With her auburn hair and smooth, pale skin, her rosebud lips and deep expressive eyes, Catherine Hewson could have sat for Titian's 'La Bella' - or perhaps his 'Venus with a Mirror'. She reminds me of Jennifer Aniston before she got too skinny. She is what my father, Leonard Stromboldt senior, calls a 'dolly bird'. He also refers to the music charts as the Hit Parade and his jeans as 'action slacks'. Dad is a model train enthusiast. But I digress.

Catherine is a nurse at St Chad's and I your humble porter. We often see each other in passing. She all trim and neat in her crisp white uniform with her long hair tied back, sensible shoes clicking on the polished floors, me hauling trains of dirty laundry or wheeling some old geezer outside for a surreptitious smoke.

Aye, you know how it is. You're lonely and a pretty girl smiles at you. You begin to compare the smiles she gives other guys with the smile she graces you. Did the raised eyebrows and half-smile she gave to Doctor Murray the ENT specialist rate more than the nodding smile to the Security man who carefully watched her reverse her little Fiat Uno in every morning? And how did the 'Good morning' and accompanying beam she flashed at me compare to the admonishing smirk she invariably posed to Doctor Capdeville, St. Chad's dental surgeon?

I made the mistake of asking Clob.

"You want to get into this bird's knickers?"

I drew a sharp breath. "There's more to it than that. Why do you have to be so base?"

"It's what I am." Clob shifted his weight on the pepper pot and fixed me with a lopsided grin. We were having this 'discussion' in the staff canteen. (It's a very small canteen - just sixteen chairs at four tables.)

"And," I continued, "I know for a fact that she doesn't put it about. She is a nice girl. Decent and respectable."

"Oh, right. You mean frigid. I can see why she appeals to you then. All your hang-ups about sex." His small eyes glinted with pure malice. "*Virgin*."

Little bastard.

I can't remember precisely how old I was when Clob first put in an appearance, but it would be when I was about fourteen or fifteen. To begin with he was a blue fish with a goggle-mask and a tank on his back full of water. I remember telling Mum about him.

"I see," she said slowly. "And what does he say exactly, this fish?"

Which was also the first question Dad, the family doctor and finally the child psychiatrist asked me. The latter, a Doctor Wilson, was a splendid black guy with a warrior build and a beautiful mellifluous voice. He is the only person I've ever met who actually had leather elbow patches on his tweed sports jacket. I looked into his noble, high-cheekboned face and began the usual question dodging. He indulged me a time before turning to my mother who was sitting beside me in this green wool coat she always wore for important occasions like Sunday worship and hospital appointments. Would she leave just the two of us together? I felt nervous myself, sure, but Mum . . . she looked panic-stricken. It was in that moment I realised something that I - with my childish self-centredness - had somehow failed to see before. Mum was weighed down with worry. No, more than worried, she was afraid.

"So we can have a nice friendly chat, Mrs Stromboldt. Man to man, so to speak."

She mouthed the words silently. *Man to man?* A frown formed on her brow.

"But he's just a boy." Then, capitulating in the face of authority, she shuffled out. It made me terribly sad.

When the door clicked behind her, Doctor Wilson moved his chair from behind the desk so he was sitting directly in front of me, our knees almost touching. "Right then, Leonard. Now that Mum is out of the room, perhaps you can tell me what this is all about." He smiled a friendly smile, the effect being slightly marred by the overhead lights reflecting on his small round glasses.

"Clob," I said helplessly.

"Clob, indeed. You said a moment ago that you can see him right now?"

I nodded.

"And what is he telling you? I want to know. I won't be angry, I promise."

I cleared my throat. "He's- he's- "

"Go on."

"He's wondering if you've got a big . . . wotsit. A big doodah." A hole yawned in front of me; I rushed to fill it with chatter. "Only he says he's heard that your sort, black men, you know, have big-"

He laid a gentle hand on my knee. "Okay, that's okay."

He tipped his head back and addressed the ceiling. "It is perfectly natural for young men to compare themselves, especially when things are beginning to develop. And if a young man was to come to me concerned about the size of his penis, afraid that somehow he didn't measure up, then I would assure him that, although there is wide variation in the size of flaccid penises, most erect penises are of similar size."

"But I didn't mean-" I swallowed the rest of the
sentence. In my dealings with adults, especially teachers
for some reason, a denial had always seemed to be taken as
proof of guilt. I sat very, very still. My cheeks were hot
enough to fry an egg.

"That may or may not be of interest to you," he said
to the room in general.

I didn't move a muscle.

He flashed me the winning smile again. "Relax,
Lenny. Can I call you that? Good. Tell me, have you ever
seen anyone else with something like Clob?"

I shook my head.

"And has anyone else ever seen Clob?"

"No." I knew where this was going. "So he's a
figment of my imagination and that's why I'm here."

"In our own time. Don't let's jump to conclusions.
Let me try something else. Have you ever heard of
Sigmund Freud, Lenny? A bit before your time, before
mine come to that, but he had a lot to say about people and
the way the mind works. Old Sigggy believed that the
psychic structure," he held up three fingers, "comprised the
super-ego, the ego and the id. The super-ego is your
conscience: all those values that you inherit from society
and your parents. The id is your basic drives, your instincts
for hunger, desire, revenge, pleasure, et cetera. And finally,
we have your ego in the middle, the part of the you which
strives to balance out the one against the other, the id
versus the super-ego."

I frowned with concentration. "You mean like, I
might want to do something that I'll enjoy, but if I know it's
wrong I won't do it?"

"Because of feeling guilty. That would be one
example, yes. Well done, Lenny." He removed his glasses
and gave them a cursory polish on his jacket lapel before
replacing them. "I'm wondering, Lenny, I'm wondering if

Clob is a manifestation of your id? Suppose that you find many of the things you think about, or like to do, make you feel guilty. I'm wondering whether the natural prurience of a young man has become a burden of guilt? If so, might you not find it convenient to disassociate yourself from that voice? Food for thought, Lenny. Food for thought." He clapped me on the knee and looked at the heavy gold watch on his wrist. "We shall talk about this more next Thursday, young man. Let's call your mum back in, shall we?"

He stood and replaced his chair behind the desk.
"What will you be missing in school?"
"Maths," I said.
"We can make it another time, if you want?"
"No thanks. Thursday's fine."

"Hey! Penny for your thoughts, Leo." Clob waved a little piggy trotter.

Doctor Wesley Wilson never did get rid of Clob. He did warn me that the idea was not to dispel Clob but to integrate him, make him a part of my natural thought processes. Much to my shame, I lied to him in the end, telling both him and my parents that Clob was no more. I should be so lucky: two years of therapy and I've still got this abusive little swine following me around more than ten years on.

"I hope you are not ignoring me, Leo."

I know he's out to rile me when he calls me Leo. I hate the way he flips it off his tongue, putting a spin on the word so that it hangs in the air long after it's uttered.

"Thinking about the fridge?"

"She is not frigid," I fumed. The trouble with arguing with a manifestation of your id is that they know every chink in your armour. "She is probably old-fashioned, and that makes a refreshing change these days." I was aware as I said it how crass it sounded.

He pursed his lips and peered over the lip of my tray.

"Didn't know you liked tomato soup?"

He'd derailed me. "Um. I don't."

"Then why, my lionhearted Leo, have you got a steaming great bowl of the stuff in front of you, hmm?"

I braced myself for further ridicule. "I've, um, I've heard Catherine is a vegetarian."

Clob sucked his fat cheeks in? "Eating that stuff will really impress her, yeah?" He made a choking sound and put a trotter to his mouth. "Now I would have thought you'd prefer a girl that likes the taste of meat, if you get my drift."

He licked his snout salaciously.

"You really are a complete bastard, you know."

"I know," he said, and sniggered. He broke off mid-snort and said, "Hey. The ice-maiden cometh."

I swallowed hard. If my careful planning came off, Catherine would sit next to me. I knew she didn't like the company of Jason Connelly, a nurse himself, and his two friends who frequented the next table, and that the tables behind me were already full. I tried to look cool.

"Hello. It's Leonard, isn't it? Do you mind if I...?"

Did I mind! "Not at all," I said, and smiled. Clob shot me a warning glance. I relaxed the face muscles. "Well," I said as she sat down to my left. "Well, well."

Clob slapped his forehead and groaned.

I went to spoon some soup up to my mouth. It ran through the tines of the fork I'd picked by mistake. I dabbed at my shirtfront with a paper napkin thinking, Jesus Christ! As I was doing so I glanced at her plate and saw what looked suspiciously like a ham salad.

"So much for that line of seduction, Leo."

I sub-vocalised something extremely rude.

"Hey, come on, Leonard," Clob smiled ruefully, "let's work at this together. I'm sorry I rubbed you up the wrong way." He looked repentant, or as repentant as a little red pig with wraparound shades, horns and a pointed tail can. "She is quite something, isn't she?"

I risked a glance at Catherine. She was daintily folding a lettuce leaf up into a compact parcel. She caught me looking at her as she popped it in her mouth, her storm-grey eyes twinkling as though she could hear my thoughts. Her complexion was like silk. "She certainly is," I said silently. "She certainly is."

A machine-gun laugh came from the next table. Stage whispering, lewd gestures and more guffawing followed it. One of the male nurses was candidly bragging to the others about his bedroom exploits by the look of things. I saw Catherine's eyes flash in annoyance. I caught her eye and tried to make it clear with a shake of the head that I too shared her disgust. I couldn't tell if she got the message.

Clob said mildly, "If you had any balls, Leonard, you'd tell those louts that there was a young lady present."

I kept my head down and cursed inwardly, knowing that what Clob said was true. But I hate to cause a scene, and I knew that the three lads would easily put me in my place if I dared caution them. I can come up with all manner of witty repartee and smouldering put-downs, but only long after the event. Anyway, I'd procrastinated too long - the moment had passed. Maybe next time. I sipped on a spoonful of soup and wished Clob would give me some useful advice.

"Hey! I'm doing my best."

Someone scraped back a chair at the table. "Is there anyone sitting here?"

"Does it look like there's anyone sitting there, you garlic-crunching pillock?" said Clob, a.k.a. Mr Tact.

"Um. No," I said, looking up into the tanned features of Doctor Capdeville. He gave me an easy smile and sat down. I saw with dismay that he had a ham salad like Catherine. It seemed terribly important.

"We've had it now, Leonard." Clob tipped his head at Catherine. "I think she's got something on with the frog."

I followed his gesture and, I must confess, I didn't like what I saw. The handsome Xavier Capdeville was clearly garnering all her attention. I took a sip of my soup. It tasted bitter.

There was raucous laughter from the next table again. Jason Connelly made a ring with a thumb and forefinger and collapsed into a fit of giggles. I didn't catch what was said but Catherine was crunching a radish with unnecessary vigour. Doctor Capdeville took the scene in instantly and, carefully putting down his knife and fork, rose from his seat. For a brief moment it looked like Catherine would object but Xavier had raised a placatory hand: *I am in charge here*, it said. He calmly went to the next table and placed the masterful hand on the shoulder of the nearest nurse. He spoke quietly in his ear, motioned to Catherine and then gently patted the shoulder again. He straightened and returned to his seat. One of the lads, looking supremely embarrassed, gave Catherine an apologetic grin before turning away. You could have heard a pin drop.

Catherine's smile was enigmatic.

"Thank you, Doctor Capdeville."

"Oh please, it's Xavier."

"You've got to hand it to the frog, Leonard. That was slick."

Xavier spoke in his heavily accented English. "The problem with English men is that they have no romance in their soul."

Clob jumped up and paced across the table. "You aren't going to let the French git get away with that are you, Leonard? C'mon, stick up for yourself!"

Xavier carried on as though he hadn't heard - because of course he hadn't.

"Love is reduced by them," he motioned to the next table, "to jokes about the meat and two vegetables, the cream horns, the wedding tackle. There is no tenderness. In France, love is an art."

I should have taken Xavier to task over his stereotyping of English manhood, but instead I busied myself with my soup, pretending I hadn't heard. Catherine, on the other hand, was more than happy to volunteer me.

"I don't think Leonard's like that. I've never heard him talking crude and I bet he knows how to treat a woman. Flowers and chocolate, stuff like that. Leonard?"

"Mm, yes, well-" I began.

Thankfully, Xavier was quicker off the mark. "I was nineteen and was dating my first English girlfriend. My family had just moved here. She was named Maria. She had this beautiful raven-black hair. I used to tell her I could see the stars reflected in it."

"Tell him, if he doesn't stop waving his fork around he'll have someone's eye out."

"She was coming up to her eighteenth birthday," Xavier continued, "a magical time in life and I wanted to get her something special."

She should be so lucky. When I was eighteen, Mum, belatedly acting on Doctor Wilson's advice to get me out socialising and interacting with others, enrolled me in the local youth club. (Dad suggested his model railway club.) Run by the local vicar, this youth club consisted of a Ping-

Pong table and a crappy little pool table with no bounce in the cushions. Fat lot of use that was. Few girls and all the lads as screwed up and repressive as me. I went to satisfy my mum's conscience for two months before I made any number of excuses to get out of it. Just as withdrawn and inexperienced with girls, I came away with a good forehand smash.

"My search for a suitable present for Maria began in the local library. I looked up the foreign language dictionaries. I remembered something about the word Maria from my Latin studies. I found it; Maria in Latin was a plural of mare. This was no help. I knew that my girlfriend loved horses but there was no way my finances could stretch that far."

"The berk! The Latin mare won't be a female horse like it is in English." Clob stumped across the table and farted in Xavier's salad.

"Mon dieu! I slapped my head! What was I thinking? *Mare* will not have the same meaning in Latin as it does in English."

"Oh, he's quick, this one. Ho hum."

"I looked it up quickly and there it was, the answer to my prayers. I began to look through other sections of the library. I now knew what I would buy my beautiful Maria. It would be perfect. Can you guess?"

"Bog off, we're not interested," said Clob.

Xavier told us anyway.

Xavier helped Maria over the stile. "I wish you'd told me we were going bloody hiking, Xav. These shoes will be ruined."

"Only a little further now, my dove."

"And it's pitch dark. Where's your torch? My dad's going to kill me if he finds out."

"Hush. We don't need a torch." A full moon bathed the hills in pools of cool limpid blues. Evening dew was forming on spider webs leaving strings of glistening pearls draped over the heather. It was ideal. He put an arm around Maria's waist and shivered with anticipation.

They followed the sandy path that wound its way up the hillside through gorse and bracken until it began to level out at the crest. "When am I going to get my surprise, Xav?"

Xavier looked at the ground around them and then up into the clear starry sky.

"Here will do."

"Here? Oh, okay. If you say so. This had better be worth it. If you've dragged me all the way up here for- for something else."

Xavier looked up at her standing there in her white stockings, pencil skirt and padded bomber jacket. She smiled and her cheeks dimpled. He raised a hand. "Come sit here beside me, Maria. I want to show you something." Maria lowered herself and patted her skirt, tugging at the hem. He guided her hands in the dark. "Here."

Maria felt at something long and slim placed in her palms. It had the feeling of leatherette and made a hollow rattling sound when she shook it.

"It's still in its case, the zip is at the top end."

"What the heck is it, Xav?" she asked, genuinely curious now. Her earlier nervousness was evaporating. The end cap came away and something cold and metal slid out. Light glinted on a glass lens. "A telescope? Lovely! Thanks. That's just what I've always wanted. This will come in useful."

Xavier laughed. "That isn't your present, Maria. You can keep it, it is for you, but it is not your present."

Maria looked at him, puzzled. All she would see in the darkness were his even white teeth and they weren't giving anything away. "I don't follow you."

"Lie back, I want to show you something."

When they were lying side by side he pointed at the moon. "Use your telescope on that. You may have to turn the ring near the eyepiece to fine focus."

Maria extended the telescope and gave a small gasp as the yellow lunar disc leapt into clearer definition.

"Wow. I can see everything."

He laughed. "That is the idea. Are you looking at the grey plains?" He snuggled closer so that his lips were near her ear. "They are called *Maria*."

"Maria? But why - I mean, what does it mean?"

"Early astronomers thought the Laval plains were water and so named them as seas, or *maria* in Latin. It's the plural of *mare* (he pronounced it muh-ray). Many have these beautiful romantic names. Do you see the large one on the left? That is *Mare Tranquillitatis*, or the Sea of Tranquillity. Slightly above is the Sea of Serenity and below is the Sea of Nectar. There are also Seas of Clouds, Showers, Moisture, Vapours . . ." He had to stop there because Maria had covered his mouth with her own. He kissed her back, deeply and slowly before gently pulling away. "All *Maria* are quite wonderful and unique in their own way," he said softly. "As are you."

He looked into eyes shiny with reflected moonlight.

Catherine's eyes were shining. "Oh, Xavier. You gave her the moon!"

Xavier Capdeville sipped at his coffee and shrugged nonchalantly.

"It was nothing," he said. His smarmy smile added, *for a Frenchman.*

"Huh, big deal. I mean, it isn't like he actually gave her anything, is it? Apart from a cheesy telescope that probably cost a couple of quid from a junk shop." Clob was trying his best but I could tell his little heart wasn't in it. I had to hand it to Xavier, there aren't many teenagers who would think of doing something like that. They tend to be more direct.

Catherine gazed at the debonair dentist over the rim of her teacup as she sipped at her drink. She put it down with a small frown. "I'd enjoy this more if I'd remembered to put sugar in."

"I'll go and get you some," I volunteered, half out of my seat.

"It's all right, Leonard," she said, placing a hand over mine, "I'm going to get myself a pudding while I'm there." She giggled conspiratorially as she rose and left the table. My hand felt warm as though indelibly imprinted by the slight pressure of her fingers.

I looked at Xavier who acknowledged me with a raised eyebrow. Our glances bounced off each other like marbles. I stared down at my soiled shirt, adjusting the lie of my tie so that it covered most of the soup stains. So much for the tomato soup gambit, I thought miserably. Had you really expected that to work? It took me a second to realise Clob's voice berating me.

"No," I sub-vocalised. I looked across to where he was sitting on the edge of the table, his chubby legs swinging to and fro. Suddenly he stood up, staring. (And when Clob stares, it's quite an event. His eyes shoot out restrained only by coiled springs that pull them back inside his head with an almighty twang. Too many wasted Saturday mornings watching cartoons, I suppose.)

"What's up? What are you looking at?" I followed his eyeballs but I could see nothing remarkable.

Clob waved a fat trotter. "That!" He looked at me, his eyebrows oscillating wildly two inches above his head. "You can't see it?"

"What?" I was starting to feel unnerved. Clob had never behaved like this before. He had never seen anything or told me anything that I, at some level, didn't already know about. This new development did not bode well.

"It's - It's his id!"

"You mean loverboy here? His actual id?"

Clob nodded, still staring at any empty patch of Formica.

I had to ask. "So. What's it look like?"

"It's a camel wearing a silver foil fez."

"A camel wearing-" That, surprisingly, didn't seem too weird. I've always associated France with Camel cigarettes ever since my Uncle George brought loads of them back from a trip to Calais. They are, I suspect, an American brand, but the association is there and the cigarettes come in soft foil packets with pyramids in the background. All this seemed to flit through my mind in a split second. I felt quite pleased at my analysis and subsequent denial.

"You are seeing no such thing, Clob."

"What d'you mean I ain't seeing no such thing? Ah, we're playing that game, are we? Ignore me and I'll go away? You never learn, do you Lenny? You gotta trust your instincts sometimes. Doctor Wilson told you that."

Catherine was settling herself down. She had chosen a strawberry cheesecake.

"Ooh, I love strawberry cheesecake," I told her.

I could faintly hear Clob protesting in the background.

"Hmm?" she said. "Oh yes, it is nice, isn't it. So, Xavier. You and Maria. Did you go out with each other for long?"

"I beg your pardon, Catherine? Oh! No. Only a matter of a few weeks."

I let my mind wander at that point. I was torn between wanting to excuse myself from the table where I had become a spare part, and staying just to be near Catherine. I chose the latter as it meant doing nothing - something I'm very good at. I watched her from the corner of my eye, her perfect lips parting as she took elegant bites from her dessert with her perfect teeth. Something in her expression made me follow her gaze to Xavier. He looked distracted, the usual easy charm and casual patter missing.

Catherine asked, "How come you parted so soon after her birthday, Xavier? I'd have thought she was very much in love with you after a gift like that." She scowled. "Some girls are so ungrateful."

The dentist shifted uncomfortably in his seat. "No Catherine, you misunderstand. It was I that finished with Maria."

He hung his head, gazing at the tabletop between his outstretched fingers. He made as if to scratch his head, paused, rubbed his eyes instead, and ended up worrying at a thumbnail with his teeth.

I glanced at Catherine, who looked at me as if she expected me to say something. I looked at Xavier to find that he too was studying me from under his fringe. I felt like an insect under a magnifying glass. I cast my eyes down to see a very smug-looking Clob. "Watch this," he said.

Xavier cleared his throat. "The point of the exercise, with the telescope and the moon, Catherine . . . " He paused to scratch a sideburn. "The point is - I only did it to get into the bird's knickers." A spasm crossed his face as though he wanted to bite his tongue off and spit it out. He dragged himself to his feet and left the table, giving me a heavy pat on the shoulder as he passed me by. His departure was as abrupt as his sordid admission.

I looked down at Clob, stunned. "You?"

He nodded enthusiastically. "Good, eh? I had a word with Humpy. Explained the situation with you and Catherine, and he had a word with the boss there. Not a bad sort for a Frenchie. Go on sunshine, the way's clear now." He tipped me a wink and popped like a soap bubble.

My eyes swivelled to take in the delectable nurse at my side. It wrung my heart to see her so. She looked like someone who had emerged unscathed from a road accident, but only by the narrowest of margins. My head was full of candyfloss with the implications of Clob and Xavier, or Xavier's id. And I was supposed to come the Casanova with Catherine? My tongue swelled to thrice its normal size and tied itself in a knot for good measure.

But I did something incredibly brave. I reached over and covered Catherine's hand with mine. She blinked, and for an awful second I thought she might snatch it away. But she didn't. *Way to go, Lenny!* Only, now what? Panic began to reassert itself. I had this vision of us sitting there all afternoon unable to break the impasse.

She said, "I really thought he was different, you know?" I gave the hand a gentle squeeze and turned my reassuring smile up a notch. "I know he has something of a reputation but, you'll laugh at me now, I thought he was honourable. I'm sick of boors like Jason Connelly. You go out with somebody like that and they are just after one thing, and after that you're just a trophy. I thought Doctor Capdeville was above that. How wrong can you be?" She indicated her plate where a lonely slice of ham was sweating. "I ordered this yucky ham salad even though I'm a vegetarian, just to have something in common with him. How sad is that?" She gave a brittle laugh and brushed a stray hair off her forehead.

"Very sad," I agreed. And then told her about the detested tomato soup. I figured it would make her feel better if nothing else.

"And here's me thinking you like the soup so much you want to take it home with you." She motioned at the stains on my shirt with her dainty chin. "So you only had soup because you thought I'd be having it? You are sweet. God, we're a pair together, aren't we?"

"Yes, we are. A pair together." The silence stretched. I still had her hand under mine. It was getting hot.

She checked the watch pinned to her breast pocket. "Oh my goodness." She pulled her hand away and made to leave. "I'm going to be in trouble with Matron if I don't get a move on."

She paused as if she was about to say something - or waiting for me to say something - changed her mind, stood up and walked away. It happened so quickly; I hadn't screwed up the courage to say my piece. I had been on the verge of asking her out. I had! So close - so bloody close - but now the moment was past and I knew with horrible certainty that I had blown my one and only chance. No! I would go after her. *Go on, Leonard.*

My traitor legs remained firmly rooted under the table. My backbone was a wet thread of cotton. Aw, who was I kidding? I slumped over the table, feeling more lonely and dejected than I could ever remember. Clob was going to give me an absolute dressing down and I would deserve every acid-coated barb he flung at me.

A voice spoke quietly at my shoulder. "My shift ends at five today." *Not now, Clob. Lay off you little -* I sat up sharply and spun round just in time to see Catherine leaving the canteen. The scent of her perfume was a lingering ghost. She popped her head round the doorframe and gave a small wave.

I think I might have waved back.

Berries Under Snow
by William M. Brock
(With thanks to A.C. Swinburne)

Nothing is better than love - not secret well water, or gemstones in a frozen sea. Although I held her hand, at death's door she cried out another's name. This only proves the pure, cold sweetness of love. God hates me for possessing it. For love, I dedicated all my soul to my Lady.

Royalty? We did not have royalty in America. We had stars plucked out of the sky. An eternity ago, I put words on the tongues of those stars.

* * *

The movie started out as another medieval epic, but the director hated every script the studio tried to pawn off on him.

"What I want," he said, "is Ivanhoe written by Edgar Allan Poe."

The producer said, "No problem." He dragged me, and my typewriter, out of a back lot shed where I wrote my page quota in the morning and drank all afternoon. They would later name an award after that efficient little man. A Russian immigrant and former bootblack, he loved hiring- owning- educated people. By his standards, I qualified. I had a graduate degree in History, had written a thesis on a nasty incident from 12th century France. I hammered out dialogue for B horror films.

The new screenplay allowed me on the set - as writer and historical consultant- to be near her. Seeing her indifference, I felt the hopeless longing that sours to hate in other men. I began a quest to find a place, any place, in her life and heart. Once, I demonstrated the proper way for a Knight to address his Lady. In Hollywoodland- the world of Kay Lynn Carter- writers are beneath notice, beneath contempt. She had no trouble showing the exact amount of disdain a royal lady would show a lowly warrior. But after the film came the reviews and the Oscar. Celestial Light created a sensation. As suddenly as that, I was a member of her entourage.

Her Ownership and my Servitude started as a game- a scene we played to amuse her friends. Soon, there was no pretense- not on my part. I found I liked being the humble writer to a rising star.

Then the stroke, lightning in my brain. Words failed me, half of my face became limp, twisted, and I could no longer be her scribe. I wore a hood to cover my deformity and brought wine and meat to her table. When she walked past, I stood so I could better see her face, the way the hair fell across her forehead. I did not sleep or eat, possessed by a waking dream of touching that hair with my own palsied hand, tasting her lips and silk eyelids with my ruined mouth.

Some memories of those dark days still bring me joy. I remember the golden hair and perfect mouth of the one she desired. I brought the girl to her arms by a hidden path.

"For myself," my Lady said, "for love, I could brave any scandal. But Kay Lynn Carter is an industry, an icon- I can't let my little peccadilloes disappoint those who think they know me so well." By the sharing of secrets, I became her confidante, the one who would not, could not betray her, bring shame to the image she protected so fiercely

She sat edgewise on the bed and told me the deepest longing of her heart - to be in reality the goddess she became on the screen. I held her tiny feet in one of my hands- such small feet - a miracle she could stand. I tried to say, "Look at your reflection in my eyes- you will see that heavenly being."

She patted my shoulder, to silence my grunting.

"Sweet Friend," she called me. I swelled with pride to be her pet, her loyal dog. But, to me, her charms were still the stuff of dreams.

Then foul disease changed her body, her face, destroyed a grandeur that shamed the night sky. A bacteria, the doctors said. They cut away parts of her to stop the wildfire infection, to save her life. It took her arm, it took her nose, and cheekbones, her cheeks (pink like the rose, soft like the rose petal) left her face a raw red chasm.

Those who swore love eternal cast her out. She was left alone- shunned and abandoned. Fools, they could not see the beauty behind the ruin.

The golden one, whose fire she had loved-who held her by the hair and devoured those over-ripe lips; she was the first to leave. The one who made my Lady sigh, and rip the night with sharp, sudden cries, who savored the hot passionate tears on her cheeks, who lay all night long in that crushing embrace while her body shuddered like the wind, rolled and bellied like the ocean. The yellow-haired beauty, skin stained red by a thousand caresses, found her a plague and ran to another's arms.

The money soon ran out - going to doctors who promised to fix what could not be fixed, restore what was lost forever. I took her to this rude cabin by the northern shore, hid her from the prying tabloids. I brought simple food and well water. I had no need of food or sleep, because I pulled back my hood and had the joy of kissing her. She wept, turning her head, shamed by the scorn she once felt for me.

My own tears fell when she asked one more sacrifice. "Sweet Friend," she said. "Please find a way for me to die."

In my vanity, I hoped she would want to live for my sake, if not her own. I began to doubt, and doubt still, if I did right. I never should have kissed her. If I had humbly provided for her needs, forgetting my own, she would have loved me more.

That was six months ago. I sit on the floor with her cold feet in my hand and gaze into her puddled eyes, the lids long ago worn away. In another realm, with new vision, perhaps she can see herself the way I see her. With my hands on her throat, she whispered the name of that golden haired girl. I fulfilled the last, most secret wish of her longing heart. That would mean something, in another kind of world.

Maybe I was a poor scribe, misreading my characters, letting the story wander to an unacceptable conclusion. I can't say I am more lonely now than before she died. Love is not so frail. It stings. It slices and reveals- a shard of broken mirror. Was she always as devoid of feeling? I want her mouth to open one more time. I want her to take a breath, move her hand, have a need I could fulfill. Then I would understand love- this glass and silver obsession.

Skin stretches over bone. Beneath the decay is the scent of acorns and black butter. The flies roar and sing a mad coda. And my need to serve her will not let me leave - it is a service God and Man forbid. Her lips are sweet, like gathered berries under fresh-fallen snow. Spider silk is not so delicate as her dry flesh. Nothing is better than love. This is what I believe.

Acknowledgements

Thanks Michael Froimowitz of Pink Stucco Press for initially encouraging this project. I also thank Ralan for http://www.ralan.com for giving us a place to petition submissions. D from Whispers of Wickedness and Adam P. Knave both provided great assistance in advice concerning publishing and distribution. Adam of Elastic Press provided inspiration. Editors Jay Lake and Thomas Deja both deserve praise for their guidance. Jay Lake, in particular, answered all of my stupid questions despite that fact that he didn't know me before I emailed him asking for advice. He helped me with Dybbuk Press as well as this particular book.

The Livejournal (http://www.livejournal.com) creators deserve a great deal of praise. Their weird amalgamation of chat rooms, mental masturbation, community building and teen angst made this book possible. Not only did I find contributors through it, but I also found many friends that helped me in many ways. In particular I'd like to thank Michael Hemmingson, Nick Kaufmann, Nick Mamatas. Their experience and professionalism helped me immensely.

Extra praise goes out to both Avi Cohen and David Gutierrez, both of whom came through when the project was on shaky ground. Also thanks to Terri Mitchem and Mary Gnetz at Lightning Source for their assistance in the publishing industry.

And of course praise goes out to the contributors. I thank them for their patience and willingness to work with me. Most of all I thank them for their contributions.

CPSIA information can be obtained at www.ICGtesting.com
Printed in the USA
BVOW072312301211

279493BV00001B/22/A